OLD FLAME, NEW SPARKS
by Day Leclaire

"There's only one excuse I can think of for Jinx bringing me in."

"And why is that?"

"Because he didn't think you were capable of handling HRI on your own," Lucas informed Kellie bluntly.

"You're wrong."

"Am I? Then explain why, after nearly two decades of marriage, your husband undercut you like this."

She knew why. But there wasn't a chance that she'd explain. "I guess you'll have to figure that out for yourself."

He approached and she fought to conceal her intense awareness of him. Why after all this time did every nerve ending seem to sizzle whenever he came near? She didn't even have to see him to sense his presence. How could one night with Lucas have created so strong a connection between them?

Dear Reader,

It is a genuine delight for me to be writing a book in Harlequin's officially licensed NASCAR series, a story that echoes the thrill and excitement of one of the best sports out there. My love for speed started at an early age, when I'd ride three-wheelers around my parents' property, raising as much havoc as I could manage. Scrapes and bruises abounded, but that never stopped me. When I turned sixteen I got not only a driver's license for cars, but one for motorcycles, as well. My dad and I would take long weekend rides on our bikes throughout the Pennsylvania hills surrounding Pittsburgh. I cherish those memories. Of course, it also earned me the high school nickname "Motorcycle Momma," something that amuses my husband to no end.

I love speed. I love the roar of engines. And I especially love being in control of both. Is it any wonder that when I discovered NASCAR I fell in love with it, as well? Now that I live in North Carolina, we tend to eat, drink and breathe NASCAR. Friends and relatives know better than to call me when a race is on! So when the opportunity arose to write this book, I jumped at it. I mean…are you kidding? Having the chance to live vicariously for several months in the NASCAR world? What could be better than that? I'll tell you what—a trip to Charlotte and getting a behind-the-scenes tour of a NASCAR NEXTEL Cup Series race. It was an unbelievable weekend and one I hope you'll get a taste of when you read *Old Flame, New Sparks!*

Please come visit me at my Web site, www.dayleclaire.com. I love hearing from readers!

Day Leclaire

//////NASCAR®

OLD FLAME, NEW SPARKS

Day Leclaire

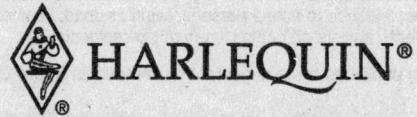

HARLEQUIN®

TORONTO • NEW YORK • LONDON
AMSTERDAM • PARIS • SYDNEY • HAMBURG
STOCKHOLM • ATHENS • TOKYO • MILAN • MADRID
PRAGUE • WARSAW • BUDAPEST • AUCKLAND

ISBN-13: 978-0-373-21779-3
ISBN-10: 0-373-21779-X

OLD FLAME, NEW SPARKS

DAY LECLAIRE

is an award-winning author of forty novels. Her passionate books offer a unique combination of humor, emotion and unforgettable characters, which has won Day tremendous worldwide popularity, and made her a member of Harlequin's prestigious "Five Star Club," with sales totaling well over five million books. She is a three-time winner of both The Colorado Award of Excellence and The Golden Quill Award. She's won *Romantic Times BOOKreviews'* Career Achievement and Love and Laughter Awards, the Holt Medallion and the Booksellers Best Award, and has received an impressive ten nominations for the prestigious Romance Writers of America RITA® Award.

Day's romances touch the heart and make you care about her characters as much as she does. In Day's own words, "I adore writing romances, and can't think of a better way to spend each day." For more information, visit Day on her Web site at www.dayleclaire.com.

In loving memory of Benny Parsons, whose warmth, wit and charm made NASCAR such a fun sport to watch, both on and off the track, and who fought the good fight with dignity and determination. We miss you!

This book would have been impossible to write without the help of some very important people. The NASCAR publishing team, particularly Emily Ross, who arranged an amazing visit to Charlotte. Nick Gallo, of NASCAR Series Operations, who gave me an absolutely fabulous behind-the-scenes garage tour. Diane Andre for her invaluable research and brainstorming assistance. To the best writing friend in the whole world, Carolyn Greene, who knows nothing about NASCAR, but listens anyway! And last but far from least, to Jada Andre. This book simply would not exist without her help. Thanks, Jada!

CHAPTER ONE

"THE RACING COMMUNITY is in mourning today following the loss of one of our most beloved personalities. James 'Jinx' Hammond, two-time NASCAR NEXTEL Cup Series champion and tireless ambassador for the sport of stock car racing, was known first and foremost for his skill behind the wheel. But when that career was taken from him in a tragic run-in with a drunk driver that left Hammond a paraplegic, he started up Hammond Racing, Inc., along with his wife, Kellie.

"This next season, watch for eighteen-year-old racing sensation, Jamie Hammond, who will bring his father's legendary Number 56 car out of retirement and show fans everywhere that the apple doesn't fall far from the tree. We extend our deepest sympathy to the friends and family of Jinx Hammond."

"I SWEAR, JINX," Kellie Hammond murmured. "I never met anyone who had worse luck than you."

What had her late husband always said? *Life has a twisted sense of humor. Me, I'm one of life's better jokes.*

She stared at his grave site where moments before a

freak snow cloud had covered up the sun and sent a minor ice-and-snow storm swirling through the crowd of mourners. The grounds had cleared out faster than pit road after a race, leaving Kellie to offer her husband a final farewell in private.

The solitude suited her. She stood within the biting embrace of the storm, her head tipped back. Snow pelted her face, mingling with her tears of grief. The icy flakes melted into her hair and the in-your-face, flame-red silk skirt and jacket she wore, an outfit Jinx had chosen personally for the occasion. Not that she cared if her clothes were ruined. She'd never wear them again.

God, she missed Jinx.

She'd never met anyone better able to find laughter in tragedy. Not when a drunk driver had confined him to a wheelchair at the height of his racing career. Not even when pancreatic cancer had cut his life short only a few months after his fiftieth birthday. A blizzard at his funeral? It was only to be expected.

"You had a bigger heart than anyone I've ever met." She dropped the silky checkered racing flag she held onto his coffin. "I'm going to miss you, sweetheart."

She sensed a presence behind her and turned, assuming she'd find her son or father standing behind her. Instead, she found the one man she least wanted to see—Lucas "Bad" Boyce.

The years had been kind to him, his black hair still rich and full, his bottle-green eyes still as direct and astute as ever. She'd first met him when he'd been a tall, lanky twenty-one-year-old. Now, pushing forty, he'd matured into one of NASCAR's most revered drivers, while still embodying the dangerous edge and air of intimidation that had earned him the nickname "Bad Boyce" that the fans and media slurred so it sounded like "Bad Boyz."

"You're going to freeze if you keep standing out in this," she said, instantly wishing she'd kept the foolish comment to herself.

He nodded in agreement, snow sinking into the thick waves of his hair and sliding down the hard-cut planes of his face. "So are you."

She shrugged. "It's just a little snow. Jinx would have found it funny. Especially the mad dash to the cars."

A slight smile touched Lucas's mouth. "Yes, he would have."

Then his smile faded as though it had never been, which was much more in keeping with the attitude he'd always taken toward her. He approached, coming to stand beside her. She'd forgotten how tall he was, how the strength of his personality surrounded him like an aura.

It amazed her that he could crawl in and out of his stock car with such ease and grace. Years of practice, she supposed, combined with a lean muscularity that left his female fan base drooling in delight. She shivered, hoping he'd put it down to the weather, rather than her reaction to him.

"Are you ready to leave?" he asked.

There wasn't anything left for her here. Jinx was

gone. Though he'd have appreciated the amazing turnout from his many friends and family, he wouldn't have wanted her standing for endless hours in the middle of a blizzard grieving his passing.

She glanced around for her son. "Jamie—"

"He left with your father." He shocked her by slipping a large, capable hand beneath her elbow. To the best of her recollection he hadn't touched her in nearly nineteen years. In fact, he'd done his best to avoid being anywhere near her. "Careful. The snow's made it slick through here."

She would have preferred to be alone, but couldn't think of a polite way of making the request, not with Lucas intent on taking charge of the situation. "I have a limo waiting."

The snow lightened as they walked, and by the time they'd reached the road, the sun slipped free from behind the cloud cover. At her approach, the chauffeur climbed from the driver's seat to open the door for her, but she waved him back. Turning to Lucas, she offered her hand. "Thank you for coming," she said formally. "Jinx would have appreciated the fine send-off."

He took her hand in his, holding it, instead of shaking it. She struggled to conceal her alarm. Surely he didn't plan to make a pass at her husband's funeral? It would be the perfect capper to the worst day of her life. "Lucas—"

He must have picked up on her distress, because he released her hand. "I know this is bad timing, Kellie, but I need to see you." He shot her a look that had her automatic protest dying before it could be uttered. "As soon as possible."

Her alarm increased. After all these years, what could he possibly have to say to her? And why now, right on the heels of Jinx's death? She could only think of one reason, one she'd prayed she'd never have to deal with.

"I'm fairly busy right now," she stalled. "With Jinx gone, I have a lot to do in order to get ready for the season. We're only two months out. Testing at Daytona is coming up in no time."

"This can't wait. Will you be at the shop tomorrow, or should I come by the house?"

"What's this about, Lucas?" she asked.

To her intense frustration, he shook his head. "Not here. Not now. It wouldn't be appropriate."

"And tomorrow would be?" She asked the question more sharply than she intended. "Lucas, you can't simply demand a meeting without explaining what's going on."

"It's business. Unfinished business between me and Jinx." He leaned past her and opened the limo door. "I'll explain everything at our meeting tomorrow."

Panic shot through her and Kellie opened her mouth to ask more questions. But one look at his face warned her she wasn't going to get anything more out of him. Lucas had always been that way. Focused, determined, hard…and that was his good side. Once the "bad" kicked in, you crossed him at your own risk.

Granted, she'd never seen him lose his temper. He

wasn't like Hammond Racing's star driver, Cole Whaling, whose explosive temper rivaled his charm and good looks. No, Lucas had a steely self-control. But that steel also made him immovable when he chose to take a stand. Clearly, this was one of those times.

"Fine," she said, caving to the inevitable. "Come to the house at one tomorrow."

He inclined his head in agreement. Then after seeing her safely ensconced in the back of the limo, he lifted a hand in farewell and disappeared in the direction of a sleek black Jaguar. It suited him, she thought. Fast, dark, dangerous.

And one hell of a ride.

SHE HADN'T CHANGED.

Lucas pulled away from the curb and eased the powerful car through its gears. How was that possible? After nearly two decades she shouldn't still look like the teenager he'd taken to his bed for that one incredible night of foolish bliss. And yet, Kellie remained one of the most beautiful women he'd ever seen.

Long, curly white-gold hair framed a heart-shaped face dominated by huge violet-blue eyes that somehow managed to hide the avarice he knew was lurking in her greedy little heart. She'd kept her figure in good shape, remaining lean and toned through the years. Granted, when he'd known her, her figure had been more coltish, more of a suggestion of the woman to come. Perhaps he should give her credit for sticking with the same man for so many years, but Lucas had been taken in by women before and considered himself a wiser man for it. Other men were weak or witless when it came to a woman like Kellie, but Lucas had lived and learned. Now in her mid-thirties, she was a woman at her most powerful and even more breathtaking, if such a thing were possible.

He'd kept his distance from her all these years, much as he'd keep a wary distance from a basking cotton-mouth on the verge of striking. But that was no longer possible. Jinx had seen to that. He'd made an offer that Lucas had found impossible to refuse, not that it had taken much thought to figure out why the offer had been tendered. From the research he'd done on the company, HRI seemed sound, with excellent people in the key positions, with one unfortunate exception.

The gorgeous, grieving widow.

Clearly Jinx didn't trust Kellie to keep Hammond Racing, Inc. running without help, despite having spent the last eighteen years of her marriage learning the ropes. It had always amazed Lucas that no one saw through her facade, though Jinx must have or he'd never have gone looking for a business partner for his wife.

Even so, it defied understanding. Those on the outside considered her one of the top businesswomen in stock-car racing. She was also adored by everyone who came into contact with her, exuding a sparkling graciousness full of warmth and sunshine, a polar opposite to his own rougher-edged personality, he conceded. Regardless, the bottom line remained the same. While Merry Miss Sunshine might prove a huge asset to both HRI and its various sponsors, if her judgment proved faulty on the business end of things, it would explain Jinx's decision.

How would she react to the information he'd present to her the next day?

Not well.

Lucas pulled onto the beltway around Charlotte and kicked up his speed, determined to curb his curiosity about her before it burrowed in and took hold. Kellie could take care of herself. She'd proven that over the years. In the meantime, he had his own plans for the future, and if he wanted to see those plans come to fruition, he'd have to maintain his focus.

He couldn't afford any distractions, particularly the sort of distractions packaged with endless legs, a figure capable of making grown men weep, the face of an angel and a puckish sense of humor. Altogether, it represented a lethal package, one he'd have to avoid at all costs. Too bad, really. Because he knew for a fact that one night with her was more heart-stopping than getting caught up in a thirty-car wreck at Talladega.

"So what did Boyce want?" Darrell asked later that evening.

Kellie didn't lift her head from her paperwork, though her father's question had the words instantly jumbling before her eyes. "Lucas?" she asked, darting him a swift glance.

"Don't know any other Boyce, do you?" Blue eyes

a shade darker than her own seemed to impale her. "I saw him talking to you on our way out of the cemetery."

"Lucas wants to meet with me tomorrow," she said with a careless shrug. Adjusting her reading glasses, she made a production of flipping through papers, hoping that would end the subject. She should have known better.

Her father's eyes narrowed. "That sounds damn peculiar. What does he want?"

"He wouldn't say." Giving in to the inevitable, she flipped the accounting folder closed and tossed her glasses to one side. "Don't worry about it, Dad. He's coming at one and I'll see what he wants when he gets here. I don't suppose you'd care to sit in on our meeting?"

Darrell's chin took on a stubborn slant. "Can't make it. Jamie and I have plans."

"Messing around with one of the old cars?"

Darrell looked momentarily chagrined. "Maybe."

"Postpone it."

"For Boyce? Not likely."

She'd known her father wasn't a fan of Bad Boyce, but he'd never said why. And because of her own history with the man, she'd never asked. Until now. "What's going on, Dad? What do you have against Lucas?"

"Why would I have anything against him?"

The question hung for an uncomfortable time. Thrusting back her chair, she crossed to his side and rested a hand on his arm. "Lucas said the meeting was business-related. He wouldn't have requested getting together if it wasn't important. Not the day after—" Her throat closed over and she didn't bother to finish her sentence.

"Can't say I'm not curious to find out what he wants," Darrell admitted. He patted her hand with a man's awkwardness in the face of a woman's tears. "But I know Bad. If he wanted me at that meeting, he'd have said so. Besides, these days I'm just a spotter. It's not like I have anything to do with the running of things around here."

"This place would grind to a standstill if it weren't for you, and you know it. And you're far more than a spotter. You were Jinx's crew chief." She gestured toward the huge window overlooking the darkened shops. "You know more about those cars than anyone on the payroll. Without you, HRI would have gone out of business years ago."

He waved her comments aside with typical modesty, before shooting her a direct look. "You sure you don't have any idea what Boyce wants?"

Her gaze flickered away. "Not a clue. Maybe he wants to buy us out. He may have won last year's NASCAR Championship, but it wouldn't surprise me if he was putting out feelers for the future, considering possibilities for when he retires from racing."

"And you think Hammond Racing is it?"

Jamie appeared in the doorway. He glanced from one to the other. "What's going on?"

She hesitated, not sure how much she should mention to her son. "Nothing much. Just a business meeting tomorrow."

He frowned. "With who? Why?"

"Lucas Boyce."

Jamie brightened. "Bad Boyce? Really? Man, I'd love to meet him."

"Meet him?" Darrell snorted. "Hell, son. In a handful of weeks you'll be racing against him."

Jamie grinned. "I can't wait. He's the best."

"Better than Cole?" Kellie asked, surprised. "I thought he was your idol."

Her son shrugged. "Cole's the greatest. But Bad's the man. Everybody knows that."

"Do me a favor and don't tell Cole that," Kellie said drily. "I guarantee he won't appreciate knowing you think he's second best. It was tough enough that he lost the NASCAR Championship to Lucas a couple months ago without you rubbing your hero worship in Cole's face."

"I wouldn't do that," Jamie protested. But a hint of chagrin showed in his expression. "So what's the business meeting about?"

The question stirred an uncontrollable anxiety, one she fought to conceal from her father and son. "I'm not sure." She offered a bright, confident smile to hide her apprehension. "I guess Lucas will explain that tomorrow."

Despite her calm acceptance of that fact, the anxiety remained, combined with a curiosity that plagued her for the rest of the evening. The only positive was that it kept her from dwelling on Jinx. It also seemed to have captured Jamie's interest. And anything that eased the sorrow from his face was well worth the torment of seeing Lucas again.

PROMPTLY AT ONE O'CLOCK, Lucas arrived. He spent the first twenty minutes dealing with Jamie's puppy-dog exuberance, patiently answering every question the youngster peppered him with, before Kellie stepped in and sent the boy on his way.

As soon as Jamie left, Lucas offered his hand to Kellie, attempting to gauge her attitude toward him. Cool to suspicious, if he were any judge. She'd also dressed for a business meeting, sweeping her hair away from her face in a simple knot and choosing a semiformal tawny brown suit accented with simple gold accessories.

"Thanks for meeting with me," he said.

"I have to admit, I'd like to know what you're doing here," Kellie replied. Her chin took on a combative jut. "There's only one reason I can think of."

Okay, not cool. Downright hostile. "And what reason would that be?"

"You're going to try and buy me out. You think that now Jinx is gone I'm going to be an easy mark?"

Lucas shook his head. "Not at all." He removed a folder from the briefcase he'd brought along and held it out.

She stared at it for a minute before accepting it. "What's this?"

"It's a contract." He didn't bother pulling his punches. It was the way he did business and most men he dealt with preferred it that way. If Kellie didn't, she was out of luck. "A contract between me and Jinx."

Kellie stared in confusion at the thick sheaf of papers she'd taken from him. "I don't understand."

Her gaze lifted to his and he winced at the expression he saw there. What was it about her? With every other woman he'd ever known, he'd been able to maintain a certain emotional distance. But not with Kellie. Never with Kellie. The only protection he'd had in his dealings with her over the years—dealings that were few and far between—had been the fact that she'd been intent on cementing her financial future by marrying a stock-car driver, no matter what underhanded method it took to accomplish her goal. Well, and the fact that she'd remained married to Jinx all these years. There were plenty of lines Lucas had blurred in his thirty-nine years. But that was one he'd never cross.

"Jinx came to me shortly after he was diagnosed with cancer," Lucas explained.

Kellie moistened her lips, betraying her apprehension. If she'd been a different type of woman, he might have gathered her up into a reassuring embrace. But the circumstances were very different, not to mention about to become extremely volatile.

"My husband signed this contract?" she replied, the question edged with disbelief. "With you?"

Lucas nodded. "I gather he didn't tell you?"

"No." She sank into the cushions of the couch behind her. "What's this about, Lucas?"

He took a seat beside her, careful not to crowd her. "In a nutshell, it's a contract to add me as a new driver to your stable."

"You must be joking! Driving what car?" she asked sharply.

"My own. The Number 121 car. That won't change. I'll still be sponsored by Wolf Sportsman."

"Why?" she demanded. "I can understand you going after Jinx when he was at his most vulnerable. He'd have made easy pickings. But why would Jinx agree to your proposal?"

He chose not to take insult at her assumption, though it was difficult. "*Jinx* approached *me*," he stated evenly. "He proposed the contract."

The words impacted like a physical blow, one she absorbed with a slight jerk. Her chin trembled for the briefest moment before she firmed it, her swift recovery impressing the hell out of him. "Again…*why?* How do I know this isn't some sort of trick or scam?"

"Your HRI lawyers helped draft the agreement and can confirm that it's legitimate and that he was the one who initiated the negotiations." He waited for that to sink in before adding, "I can't say why he made the offer. He refused to explain. I was hoping you could tell me."

For some reason the question elicited a powerful reaction. Her eyes widened and every scrap of color drained from her face. "I have no idea," she claimed.

It was a lie. He couldn't say how he knew, but there wasn't a doubt in his mind. He didn't bother calling her on it. There'd be plenty of time for that when they started working together. "There's more," he said.

She thrust a hand through her hair in tired frustration, loosening the knot so curls spilled in delightful disarray around her face. "Of course there is." She visibly steeled herself. "What else?"

"An old family friend approached me while I was in contract negotiations with Jinx. He wanted to be the main sponsor for the 121, but I was forced to pass since I have a long-term contract with Wolf. I nudged him toward Jinx since I heard the Number 56 car was looking for sponsorship."

"Jamie?" she asked, surprise clear in her voice. "You suggested a sponsor for Jamie's ride?"

Lucas nodded. "After meeting with Jinx they were really excited. The Number 56 car has quite a history and they liked the idea of coming onboard to help bring the number out of retirement. The publicity from that alone should make it well worth their investment."

Some of her apprehension faded, replaced with delight. "That was very generous of you, Lucas." At his hesitation, her eyes narrowed. "Okay, I know that look. There's a 'but' in there, somewhere. What is it?"

"The sponsor is Food Basket."

"Jamie's already partially sponsored by Gold's Supermarkets."

"Gold's is a small regional chain. Food Basket is national."

"And has a non-compete clause, I'll bet."

Lucas nodded. "Gold's will have to go." He held up a hand when she started to argue. "There's nothing to discuss, Kellie. You know it and I know it. Gold's can't offer anything close to what Food Basket can and Food Basket won't allow one of their main competitors in this region of the country to have their name splashed across the same car."

"Gold has been with us since the start," she protested. "They kept us going, almost single-handedly, after Jinx's accident. They've also sponsored some of Cole's rides since we brought him onboard."

"It's all about the bottom line. And the bottom line says Gold's can't bring in the money Food Basket can. I'm sorry, Kellie."

Her mouth took on a stubborn slant. "Did Jinx know about this?"

"Yes. We worked the deal together."

He'd never seen her appear so devastated. "Why didn't he tell me?"

Since she'd asked, he gave an honest opinion, not bothering to soften it. "I suspect for the same reason he didn't tell you about any of this. He was too weak to fight you over his decisions."

She closed her eyes. This time she didn't bother to hide her pain and sorrow. "Did he tell you that?" she whispered.

Lucas shook his head. "He didn't have to. These are huge changes, Kellie. I'm guessing he knew you'd resist them. A new driver, a new sponsor, having to drop your old one…"

He wasn't through. He hadn't mentioned the final change, and this next part would hit her hardest of all. He could walk out and leave her in the dark. But he didn't want her to read the contract and discover it that way. Better to give her all of it, every last nasty clause.

"One last thing…" he began.

"You have to be kidding." A hint of bitterness crept into her voice. "This isn't bad enough?"

He lifted an eyebrow at that. "You think it's bad to have me in your stable? To have a new sponsor of Food Basket's caliber?"

"No, of course not. It's how—" She broke off, no doubt before she said something disloyal about Jinx. "What else, Lucas?"

He leaned forward, resting his forearms on his knees. He'd rather not be this close to her, so close he could inhale the sweetness of her perfume. But he wanted to watch her reaction, just as he wanted her to see how determined and immovable he'd be in regard to every part of what he was about to reveal. "This next part directly impacts HRI and my role within the company."

She didn't get it, not at first. "Your role as a driver?" She released her breath in a gusty sigh. "You mean perks, don't you? Darn it all, Lucas. Just how much did you finagle out of Jinx?"

"This has nothing to do with my role as a driver and everything to do with my role as a business partner."

She shook her head in denial, but he could see comprehension hovering on the periphery of her expression. "I don't understand," she choked out.

"Then let me spell it out for you. Shortly after Jinx was diagnosed with cancer, he sold me forty-nine percent of the business, to take immediate effect the day after his funeral. That's today."

CHAPTER TWO

KELLIE FOUGHT TO BREATHE. "No. He wouldn't have done that."

"He would and he did," Lucas corrected. He mentioned the price he and Jinx had agreed on, a fairly hefty number, but a fair one. "The funds sit in an escrow account until the end of the season. At that point there are three options, all within my control and at my discretion. Option one, I can collect my toys and walk away. The money reverts to me and you continue as you did before my advent. Option two, I elect to continue as your partner, maintaining the status quo, with you holding the majority shares of HRI."

"And option three?" As overwhelmed as she was by all the information he'd thrown at her, she couldn't believe she had sufficient brain cells to ask.

"Jinx offered me a bit of a sweetener."

"You must be joking! This outrageous deal you foisted on him isn't sweet enough already?" It took every ounce of self-possession to regain her self-control instead of continuing to vent the emotions clawing for escape. Years of practice came to her rescue, allowing her to hold onto her dignity, if only by a thread. But at least it held. "Finish it, Lucas. What's the sweetener?"

"If I win the NASCAR Championship again, I have the option to purchase an additional two percent of HRI, giving me controlling interest." There was no mistaking his satisfaction. "Fair warning, when I win the championship this coming season, I'll be exercising that option."

Kellie shot to her feet and paced to the far side of the room before spinning to face him. "Controlling interest." How could Jinx do this to her? He'd not only allowed the object of her greatest despair to wander in and take up residence on her couch, he'd *invited* Lucas in. Well, if Bad Boyce thought she'd simply surrender and allow herself to be forced into submission, he was in for a surprise. She lifted her chin and regarded him coldly. "At least Jinx didn't sell cheap."

Lucas acknowledged her swift recovery with a fleeting smile. "No, you didn't come cheap." Before she could respond to the suggestive taunt, he continued. "You'll get your money's worth, both from having me on your team, as well as from our partnership."

"Is that all of it?" she demanded. "Are there any more clauses I should know about? Any more surprises?"

"That's all of it." He stood. "I advised Jinx to tell you about the contract, but he wouldn't hear it. Maybe he didn't want his last few months to be contentious. And they would have been, wouldn't they? I suspect you'd have fought tooth and nail to keep him from selling out."

"Wouldn't you have?" She turned some of her anger

in his direction. "Jamie should have inherited HRI. How am I supposed to explain his father's decision when you take the business from him?"

Anger gleamed in Lucas's green eyes. "Jamie's only eighteen. In February he's going to climb into a stock car carrying his father's old number in the toughest, most competitive racing venue there is. He's not capable of running HRI and won't be for decades, and we both know it. So, answer me this, Kellie. Are you really upset that I 'stole' Jamie's inheritance?" He walked to the door and paused there long enough to spare her a final look. "Or your own?"

He didn't wait for her response, but left her standing there staring at his retreating back.

"ANYONE WHO THOUGHT Silly Season had ended when Lucas 'Bad' Boyce won this year's NASCAR NEXTEL Cup Championship hasn't heard the latest news coming from the Boyce camp. Just today it was announced that Bad Boyce will become Hammond Racing, Inc.'s premier driver, increasing HRI's stable of talent to three 'dream teams.' Even more astonishing, he's purchased an astounding forty-nine percent of HRI.

"Expect sparks to fly when HRI's star, Cole Whaling, is obligated to share quarters with the man who snatched the NASCAR Championship away from him, forcing him to swallow the title of 'second best.' And expect those sparks to burst into flames when gorgeous businesswoman Kellie Hammond has her every move second-guessed by her new partner. Stay tuned, fans!"

"THAT SON OF A——"

"Stop it, Cole!" Kellie cut him off before he could launch into a full-blown tirade. The rest of the team and staff members sat around the conference table in watchful silence, listening avidly to their argument. "You're not helping. It's a done deal and nothing any of us can say will change that. The contracts were signed before last season even ended. All that's left to do is try and make the best of it."

The driver glared at her, his hazel eyes gleaming with anger. Usually, he was Mr. Charm, himself. Charismatic. Boyish. Witty. With a flash of his deep-set dimples he'd always managed to get anything he wanted. Or anyone. At least, he was careful to maintain that facade in public. But in the decade he'd been Jinx's premier driver, she'd learned that you crossed Cole at your own risk.

"We can argue Jinx wasn't of sound mind when he signed the contract," Cole suggested. "Your lawyers should be able to find a loophole."

"My lawyers, in case you've forgotten, were also Jinx's. They're the ones who drafted this contract. It's legally binding. And if you think I'm going to try and invalidate Jinx's last wish, let me disabuse you of that notion right here and now."

"You're going to just sit back and let him take over?"

It infuriated her that he was stirring up dissension in front of the others. She should have anticipated that and cut him off before he'd worked up a full head of steam. "Boyce isn't taking over anything. Yes, he's now my partner. But he's a driver, the same as you and the same as Jamie. I maintain controlling share of the business. My decisions will be the final ones."

"For now," Cole said. "If he wins the NASCAR Championship this next year, he'll own a controlling share. He could replace you. Hell, he could kick you out and take over your job."

She'd already thought of that. "We'll deal with that if and when it happens."

Cole kicked back his chair. "I suggest you start thinking of a way out now, before he takes this place down."

Kellie slapped her hands against the conference table. "You're being ridiculous. Why would he want to take HRI down, even if he could?"

"I don't know. Do you?" Cole turned to face her, his eyes narrowed. "Any old grudges? Any reason Bad Boyce would want to harm HRI?"

Oh, God. It took every ounce of control to maintain her cool. "Not a one. Lucas is coming onboard because it's an excellent career opportunity for him. HRI is a strong company. We were second in the NASCAR Championship this past season. We're about to launch a new driver who'll be behind the wheel of one of the most revered numbers in the sport. The media attention from that alone is worth the price of admission. And Lucas knows it. Knows it and wants a piece of it."

Cole's lip curled. "You mean, he wants a place to finish out his career."

"He's not exactly a has-been, Cole. He's only a

couple of years older than you *and* he beat you out for the championship. I don't think he's going to be parking his ride anytime soon."

"Not until he wins this year's NASCAR NEXTEL Cup Championship and takes over as owner of HRI."

"Enough." She shoved back her chair and stood. Her gaze scanned the various team members and personnel she'd instructed to attend this meeting. "I asked all of you here to give you an update. Lucas is going to be moving in over the next week. I don't want any trouble. We're going to be a family—even if it kills us."

The door to the conference room opened just as Cole cut loose with a word that, even after all her years around rough-tongued men in garages, left her shocked. To her horror, Lucas stood there and one look warned he was far from happy.

"Interrupting something?" he asked with deceptive calm.

"Not at all, Lucas." She slammed a hard-won detachment in place and modulated her voice to reflect it. "Please come in. I was just explaining to my employees the recent changes and additions to HRI."

"Our. Our employees." His gaze shifted to Cole and chilled perceptively. Then his attention shifted to the rest of the gathering. "If you'll all excuse us…?" En masse, those seated at the conference table erupted from their chairs and made a beeline for the door. When Cole started to follow, Lucas shifted to block him. "You can go after you apologize for your language."

Cole stared in disbelief, his hands balling into fists.

"You're joking." When Lucas continued to stand there, Cole shook his head. "Forget it. That's not going to happen."

Lucas didn't actually move, yet it seemed to Kellie that he grew in size, appearing larger and tougher and more dangerous than she'd ever seen him. "Oh, it's going to happen. It's just a matter of whether it'll happen with you standing up like a man, or on the floor clutching a broken nose. Doesn't make much difference to me which way it goes down." And then he smiled, a feral baring of his teeth. "Who am I kidding? Laying you out would make my day."

The standoff lasted a full thirty seconds before Cole caved. "Sorry if I offended you, Kellie." He shot her a swift, furious look over his shoulder. "Remember what I said. You can't claim I didn't warn you."

The instant the door closed behind him, Kellie turned on Lucas. "How dare you?"

He regarded her with nearly the same amount of fury as he had Cole. "Funny, I was about to ask you the same question. You'll have to get used to sharing the head of the table with your new business partner. From now on I'm to be included in all HRI business meetings. Got it?"

How had he managed to put her on the defensive with such ease? "I was simply explaining the changes that will be occurring."

He lifted an eyebrow at that, honing in on the one flaw in her argument. "Since you don't know what changes to expect, how can you inform our employees?"

"They needed to be warned," she insisted doggedly.
"Warned?"

She waved that aside. "Fine. Told."

"And I should have been there when you told them.
That way we could have presented a unified front, as
partners, while dealing with any questions they had.
That way you could have avoided Cole's causing dissension with that outburst of his. I only caught a portion
of it. I'm sure there was a lot more that was a lot worse."

"He'd still have complained."

"But not in such a public forum. And not in a way
that left our employees worried about HRI's future. The
start of the season is only weeks away. We need
everyone with their head in the game, not second-
guessing management."

She hated that he was right almost as much as she
hated how he stirred a heat in her unlike anything she'd
felt in years, putting her at an immediate disadvantage.
She needed to stop this, and fast. If she didn't want him
running roughshod over her, she'd have to set the tone
for the future right from the start. "They're very clear
about who's in charge, Lucas. I am. As the majority
owner, the final decision on every aspect of this business
rests with me."

"For now."

She inclined her head. "Unless and until that changes,
I'm happy to listen to what you bring to the table. But I'm
not about to let you bully me into doing things your way."

He folded his arms across his chest. "Don't count on
that."

"Excuse me?"

"There's only one reason I can think of for Jinx bringing me in."

He'd caught her off guard with his comment and she regarded him with instinctive wariness. "And why is that?"

"Because he didn't think you were capable of handling HRI on your own," Lucas informed her bluntly.

Even though she knew it wasn't true, she couldn't prevent a wave of pain from ripping through her. "You're wrong."

"Am I?" He tilted his head to one side. "Then explain why he sold out to me. Why, after nearly two decades of marriage, would your husband undercut you like this? What possible motivation could he have?"

She knew why. Or at least she had a strong suspicion. But there wasn't a chance in hell that she'd explain the reason to Lucas. "I guess you'll have to figure that out for yourself. Now, are we finished here?"

"We are, assuming we have an understanding about how we're going to handle future business meetings."

He approached and she fought to conceal her intense awareness of him. Why, she wondered in despair? Why after all this time did every nerve ending seem to sizzle whenever he came near? She didn't even have to see him to sense his presence. He'd proven that year after endless year, though she doubted she'd ever betrayed any hint of her reaction to him or anyone else. Except, she realized now, to Jinx. She'd never understood it.

How could one night with Lucas have created so strong a connection between them?

"We do understand each other, don't we?" he asked. "Partners make business decisions together. As far as the team members and staff are concerned, we're one big happy family."

"You're pushing it." More than anything she wanted to fall back before his approach. But she couldn't allow him that much control. She held her ground despite the overwhelming urge to give in and give up. God, she was tired. "I have a lot of practice putting on a happy face, but no one's going to believe we're that close, let alone happy."

"I'm well aware of that. Say what you want to me in private, but in public we speak as one." His hand settled lightly on her waist before sliding downward, following the womanly flare of her hip and squeezing. "When it comes to outsiders, you and I are joined right here. Hip to hip."

She met his knowing gaze with as much equanimity as she could manage. "Take your hands off me."

"It's been a long time, hasn't it, Kellie?"

"You no longer have the right to touch me. Ours is a business relationship and nothing more." She took a deliberate step backward, forcing his hand to fall away. "Are we clear?"

"Quite. I'm just relieved that you realize that fact, too. Our situation is difficult enough without complicating it."

"Then…" She couldn't help brushing at her hip as though to remove his touch. "Why?"

"Curiosity, plain and simple." He smiled enigmatically. "I had a question, which you've now answered."

The comment left her totally confused, but before she could demand an explanation, he exited the conference room, stepping aside so Jamie could enter. Her son only waited for the door to close before jumping in with typical directness.

"Bad can't really take HRI away from us, can he?" Jamie demanded.

"No, of course not," Kellie said, quick to reassure him. She fought to switch gears, though with her heart still pounding from the warmth of Lucas's hand, it was difficult.

"But if he wins the NASCAR Championship…"

She fought to conceal her exhaustion at having to explain the facts for the umpteenth time. "Then he'll own fifty-one percent of HRI—at a hefty price, I might add. We'll still retain the other forty-nine."

"But Cole's right. That'll mean Bad will be in charge."

Kellie crossed to her son's side and rested her hand on his shoulder. When had he gotten so tall? It seemed like just yesterday that the top of his head had been at perfect kissing height. "We have a full racing season ahead of us before we have to worry about that. Do you know how difficult it is to win the championship once, let alone twice in a row?"

"But it's Bad Boyce. He's—" Jamie's blue eyes shone for an instant with unmistakable hero worship before anger eclipsed every other emotion. "He's the best there is. If he wins one more championship, it'll give him his eighth. That'll be a NASCAR record. Do you know how much incentive breaking that record will give him?"

Knowing Lucas, too much. "Even the best isn't the best all the time. Listen to me, Jamie. Lucas will be a tremendous asset to HRI. I know how much you're missing your father, how difficult this next year will be without him to guide you. But Lucas will be able to teach you a lot. Give him a chance."

She could see the conflict in her son's face. Until a few years ago, Jamie had papered his room with posters of favored race car drivers, with Lucas holding a prominent position. But as much as he worshipped Lucas, he also admired Cole, something the older driver took full advantage of. She suspected Jamie wanted to side with Cole on the subject of Bad Boyce, even while part of him was thrilled at the idea of working with the NASCAR NEXTEL Champion.

"Give him a chance, Jamie," she repeated. "See how it goes."

"Are you going to give him a chance?" he shot back. "I heard you and Paps talking. You're not happy about his being here, either."

"I'm not happy about the way it went down," she admitted. "But having him associated with HRI will be great for business. Plus, he's brought along a fantastic sponsor for you." She ruffled her son's chestnut hair, something she didn't dare do in public, and edged their discussion in a new direction. "We'll be meeting with

Food Basket at the end of the week. They want to unveil the new color scheme for your car and discuss photo ops and promos. You're about to hit the big times, kiddo. You ready?"

Jamie didn't hesitate. He shot her a look of such drive and determination that for a split second it might have been his father standing before her instead of their son. "Yeah, I'm ready. Racing is all I've ever wanted to do."

"I know."

"I'm going to be the best, Mom. You wait and see. I'm going after a NASCAR Championship and nothing and no one is getting in my way."

Kellie watched as her son exited the conference room. There was no question, she realized with a shiver. Jamie was definitely his father's son.

JAMIE WALKED OUT of the conference room, exuding as much self-confidence as he could manage. That's what his mother wanted to see…heck, what they all wanted to see—that he was upbeat and sure of himself. But it wasn't the truth. At least, not the entire truth.

He wandered outside, past the shops that housed his car and Cole's 199, toward an older garage where some of his father's legendary 56 models were kept. He flipped on the overhead spots. The light seemed to shoot from car to car, causing the distinctive green and gold colors to flash like lightning.

Here was the car his father drove when he won at Daytona. Jinx had been more proud of that win than any other. Of course, the next three years, he'd crashed on the last lap—the "Hammond Jinx" at its worst. Then there was the Thunderbird he'd been driving when he won his second and final NASCAR NEXTEL Cup Championship, not long before a drunk driver had put an end to a career at its zenith.

He climbed into the Daytona winner and rested his head against the steering wheel. Some of his earliest memories were of sitting in this car, so small he couldn't even see out of the windshield. How many imaginary races had he driven and won from the seat of this car? But he wasn't dealing with imagination anymore. This was the real deal. And one question, more than any other, continued to plague him.

He knew he'd inherited the Hammond drive and determination, the "want to." But what else had he inherited? The Hammond Skill…or the Hammond Jinx?

"Jamie?"

"In here, Paps."

His grandfather entered the garage. "Thought this might be where you were. You always crawl in that old car when something's troublin' you. What is it this time, son?"

Jamie shrugged. "Just missing Dad, I guess."

His grandfather's expression softened. "We all miss him. It's not going to be the same without him."

"I'd hoped—" To Jamie's horror, his voice cracked and he fought to bring it under control. "I'd hoped he'd be there to see me race at Daytona."

"Trust me. He'll be watching."

"What if—"

"If…what?" Darrell prompted.

Jamie shook his head. Putting it in words might make it real instead of keeping it stomped down into just a vague fear. "Nothing. Never mind."

His grandfather tapped the roof of the car. "Well, enjoy your last ride in there, son. I'll see you back at the house for dinner."

"What? Wait a sec." Jamie yanked off the steering wheel and tossed it to one side before levering himself out of the window. "What do you mean, last ride?"

Darrell grimaced. "Aw, hell. I thought you knew. Well, better you hear it from me, I guess." He released his breath in a gusty sigh. "These cars are going to be moved to the museum next week."

"Why?"

"We need the space for Lucas."

Jamie thrust a hand through his hair. No. It couldn't be. "Because of Boyce? They're getting rid of Dad's cars because Bad Boyce is moving in? He's taking over Dad's garage?"

Darrell dropped a hand on Jamie's shoulder. "Easy, son."

"No." He shrugged off his grandfather's hold. "This place belongs to Jinx Hammond. *The* Jinx Hammond. Boyce can park his ride someplace else."

"There is nowhere else, and you know it. Listen to me, Jamie. Having Boyce here will be good for business. It'll be good for you, especially with Jinx gone. There's no one driving today who's better than Bad."

"Cole. Cole is as good."

Darrell shook his head. "He's close. But he's not as good. Think on it, son. You'll have two of the most experienced drivers the NASCAR NEXTEL Cup Series has to offer as your teammates."

"But here?" Jamie looked around him, feeling desperation seizing hold. "It'll be like Dad never was."

"Your father built this place. He will always be a part of it. Nobody can take that away."

"Boyce will try." Jamie's mouth tightened, anger grabbing him. "But I won't let him. He's not getting his hands on HRI. Not while I have anything to say about it."

"Now listen to me, son. You stay out of all that legal wrangling. That's for Boyce and your mother to deal with."

"But if he wins the NASCAR Championship…"

"It was Jinx who put that provision in there." He made the point deliberately. "Think it through, Jamie. Your father was one of the most stubborn men I ever knew. There were days when I wasn't sure why anyone bothered to call me Jinx's crew chief since he didn't listen to a word I had to say. If your father hadn't wanted that condition in there, he'd never have agreed to it. Period. End of discussion."

"But why?" Jamie asked desperately. "Why'd he do it?"

"We may never know." A gleam appeared in eyes the same violet-blue as Jamie's own. "Or we may find out down the road a piece. Your father always did have a wicked sense of humor. Time will tell if this is his idea of a joke. Until then you have a job to do and it isn't snarling over Boyce setting up shop here."

"But Cole says—"

"Cole makes a habit of talking out of places that shouldn't have mouths."

Jamie grinned. "And where would that be, Paps?"

"You oughta know. You've made that same mistake a time or two, yourself." Darrell smiled at his grandson. "Take your time in here. I'll make your excuses to your mother."

"Thanks."

Jamie looked around after his grandfather had left. So much history. So many memories. But nothing stayed the same forever. The cars in here had been the best of the best a couple of decades ago. Now they were antiques. His father was gone, though his number would live on—depending on Jamie's skill and success. It was time to take from the old to build something new.

"Goodbye, Dad," he whispered, and turned off the lights.

LUCAS MOVED HIS CARS and team into HRI exactly one week later.

Kellie stood at the window of her office and watched the hauler and moving van pull up, followed closely by a distinctive black Jag. She'd arranged for her general manager to help Lucas's team get comfortable in their workplace. But it was her job to welcome her "premier" driver and business partner, as news reports were now describing him.

Exiting her office, she left the building housing the shops and waited on the outskirts of the crowd that milled around the yard as they greeted the new arrivals. After twenty minutes, people dispersed, returning to their various jobs. Kellie approached Lucas and offered her hand.

"Welcome," she said simply.

Unfortunately, the sensations that rocketed through her when he took her hand were far from simple. She wanted to yank free of his grasp, but didn't dare for fear it would give too much away. And it was that "too much" that worried her.

She shouldn't be feeling like this when Lucas touched her, shouldn't feel anything for him, anymore. Not after all these years. It was dangerous, a threat to the life she'd built with Jinx, as well as the life she hoped to continue from this point forward. How was she supposed to maintain a professional distance now that he'd joined HRI, when every time he looked at her or touched her, she reverted to a hormone-crazed seventeen-year-old? The worst part was…how was she going to get through the endless weeks and months of the upcoming season?

She was his partner and all she could think about was getting him horizontal and having her wicked way with him. Again.

"You can let go now," Lucas said mildly.

It took her a split second to figure out what he meant.

The instant she did, she snatched her hand free of his. "Sorry. I'm a bit preoccupied at the moment."

"I can understand. A lot's happened in a short period of time." But the knowing smile he offered seemed to cut straight through her excuses. "Why don't you show me where we'll be parking our cars."

"Of course."

She took him through the shop, taking ridiculous pleasure in his appreciation of the size and scope of the work area. Once he'd fully acquainted himself with his new home, she ushered him into the private office she'd cleared out for his use. "You can use this, since it's convenient to the shop, or there's something a bit grander near my office. I assume you have your own furniture," she continued. "If not, order whatever you need."

"Thanks." He leaned against the door frame, blocking her exit, and studied her in a way that had her nerves firing in reaction. He'd grown so intimidating over the years, exuding a toughness that made his nickname fact as much as legend. "Maybe this would be a good time for the two of us to have a private conversation."

Oh, dear. Fighting nervousness, she offered her calmest, most professional smile. "About what?"

"The present. The future." His focus tightened, laser-sharp. "Or maybe we should start with the past."

CHAPTER THREE

KELLIE SNATCHED a deep breath and fought to return his look with as much composure as she could scrape together. But he'd shaken her, and chances were excellent he knew it. "Fine. Let's talk about the past. As far as I'm concerned, it can stay where it belongs. Behind us. I have no interest in resurrecting a dead issue." And she hoped to heavens that Lucas shared that disinterest.

He continued to hold her with a sharp, penetrating stare, which pretty much put an end to those hopes. It would seem that their one night together was still a subject of concern. At least, for him. "I've always wondered something about that night," he told her. "Did it matter which driver you tempted into your bed?"

She could feel herself pale. "I was no 'pit lizard,'" she snapped, employing the term the team used for women who cruised the garages in the hopes of snapping up a "name" for a bit of action. "I was a foolish child, suffering from an even more foolish crush. Now, if you wouldn't mind I'd—"

He shook his head. "It was more than that and you know it. I'm well aware that you weren't just racking up your first notch on your bedpost. You wanted the whole package, didn't you? Marriage, the reflected glory." His eyes hardened. "A baby to ensure a healthy divorce settlement."

She laughed. She had no idea where it came from. But it saved her from disaster, bursting from her in glorious, genuine amusement. "Get over yourself, Bad. You were my first mistake, if not my last. If I was the sort of person you claim, I'd have divorced Jinx long ago and taken him for every penny I could. Instead we were happily married for eighteen years. Are you sure you're not coloring me with Bridgette's brush?" she asked, referring to his ex-wife.

He conceded her point with a shrug. "Then how did you end up with Jinx so soon after our night together?"

She'd anticipated this question. Planned for it. "I realized I'd made a terrible mistake sleeping with you." That much was true enough. She'd imbued Lucas with qualities she'd wanted in the man she'd love and marry, rather than with those he actually possessed. She'd created a fairy tale out of reality and tried to cast him in the role of Prince Charming. It not only hadn't worked, it had been an unmitigated disaster. But along with that single truthful statement came the lie she desperately hoped to sell as truth. "I also realized that I was using you as a stand-in for the man I really wanted. Jinx."

Lucas took a moment to consider her words before pushing a bit harder. "Your father must have had a thing or two to say about your relationship with Hammond, especially when you were all of seventeen and he was a solid fifteen years older. Not to mention being a paraplegic." Lucas's eyes narrowed in thought. "He was hit by that drunk driver just a few weeks after we were together, wasn't he?"

"Yes." She managed to shove out that single word, but adding to it proved beyond her.

"You must have conceived Jamie during those two weeks, since you were clearly pregnant by the time Jinx left the rehab hospital. I mean, you were adamant that the baby wasn't mine when I asked."

"Jinx and I married the day he was released," she said, confirming his one assumption, without bothering to address the others.

Lucas continued to block the office door or she'd have shoved past him and put an end to the discussion. If she had a hope of dealing with him on any sort of an equal footing, she needed to stand up to him, no matter how difficult.

She allowed a hint of impatience to bleed into her voice. "What's the point of all this, Lucas? Why dredge up ancient history? I think we can both concede that I was an idiotic seventeen-year-old. But that was ages ago."

"I'm well aware of how long ago it was." Something in his comment snagged her attention, but before she could analyze it, he continued. "I'm wondering why you slept with me. You were a virgin, and yet there's no question in my mind that you came after me that night at the party. Granted, I was more than happy to accommodate you."

"Until the next morning."

Wry acknowledgment swept across his expression.

"And woke up to discover that the sophisticated twenty-year-old I'd taken to bed had transformed into a girl not yet out of high school."

The years had turned that soul-deep pain into a gentle ache, enabling her to handle the memory without the anguish that had threatened to tear her apart back then. "Not to mention being Darrell Reynolds's daughter."

He winced. "That alone guaranteed the end of my career if anyone had found out. I kept expecting Darrell, Jinx and the entire shop and team to come after me when they found out what I'd done to you and dole out a serious hurting."

"And they would have been all too happy to do some doling...if I'd ever told them we'd had a one-night stand."

"Which brings me back to my original question." She thought she'd managed to ease him away from that, but she should have known better. Lucas had always possessed infinite focus, something that had contributed to his success on the track. "I keep wondering why, Kellie. Why me? And why didn't you ever tell anyone what we'd done?"

She looked him straight in the eye and lied for all she was worth. "Because Jinx was the man I loved, but my father would have cut him to pieces if he'd tried anything with me. So, I turned to you because I thought you were the next best thing. But you weren't." She couldn't help the taunt. "You aren't anything like Jinx, are you?"

Lucas shook his head, his expression settling into grim lines. "No, I'm a very different man."

"So I found out." She folded her arms across her chest. "Are we done with all this now? Can we finally leave the past where it belongs…in the past?"

"Sure." He waited a beat before adding, "That just leaves the present and the future."

She fought to keep from reacting, to keep a pleasant expression on her face and any hint of despair from reflecting in her eyes. "That's easy enough. You're my partner, as well as one of my drivers. Since you were so quick to list your expectations the last time we spoke, I'll return the favor." She ticked off on her fingers. "I expect you to fulfill your contractual commitments and attend all the pre- and post-race meetings. I expect you to keep all internal disagreements out of the media and work on getting maximum exposure for your sponsors and HRI. I expect you to give your usual one hundred percent to winning races. And most of all, I expect you to play nicely with the other drivers."

He appeared intrigued by one of the items on her list. "You sure you want me to give a hundred percent to winning?"

It only took an instant to understand what he meant. "Do I want you to win another NASCAR Championship? Actually, I would." She gave him a brilliant smile. "Next year."

His grin cut deep grooves on either side of his mouth. "In that case, I only have one last question."

Relief made her cocky. "Hit me."

"How do you plan on dealing with what's going on between us?"

Her smile died. How did he do it? One minute she felt secure in the knowledge that they had a shot at maintaining a strictly business relationship, and the next he had her wanting to tumble into his arms. Well, she wouldn't let him get away with it. She hit him with her coldest glare. "And what do you imagine is between us, Lucas?"

He straightened away from the doorjamb and approached. Could he tell how difficult it was for her to keep her knees locked in place? Considering the hint of amusement that drifted through his black gaze, he did. He drew to a stop a scant few inches away. For a race car driver, he was unusually tall, a solid six foot two worth of powerful male. He didn't attempt to pull her into his arms as she half expected. Instead, he reached out with a single finger and dragged it along her cheek to the edge of her mouth before tracing her lower lip.

She closed her eyes, hiding from what she couldn't handle. Reaction slammed through her, and a hot, tight ball of desire knotted low in her belly while a forbidden need sizzled through her veins. How was it possible that she still wanted him? That with one touch, she'd be willing to put herself right back where she'd been eighteen years ago? Unbidden and unwanted, the tiniest of moans escaped her and her eyes flew open in horror.

A flame ignited in his gaze at the telltale sound. "That," he murmured. "That's what's still between us. And I've had a hankering for another taste for eighteen long years."

Without another word, he turned and headed for the door.

He exited the office, leaving her totally undone.

"THE EXCITEMENT IS heating up. We're just a few short weeks from Daytona and fans are counting the days until the NASCAR NEXTEL Cup season takes its first green flag. It's crunch time and all eyes are on Hammond Racing, Inc. and its stellar racing teams.

"Will Bad Boyce kick off the season by making an early grab for the points lead as he races toward a repeat NASCAR NEXTEL Cup Championship? Or will Cole Whaling, Bad's new teammate and Championship runner-up, decide he doesn't like being second best? Or will HRI newcomer Jamie Hammond surprise us all, showing off the driving chops he undoubtedly inherited from his father? Fans who want to see Jamie's brand-new uniform and race car paint scheme will get the opportunity at Food Basket's shindig in two short weeks, where everyone who's anyone will be celebrating the official unveiling.

"In the meantime, rumors swirl that the three HRI drivers aren't playing as nicely as team owner Kellie Hammond might like. Three rowdy boys, all after the same prize. What's a mother to do? I'll tell you what you should do. Stay tuned for the latest breaking news and racing updates!"

LUCAS SPOTTED HER the instant he walked into the reception area.

There was something about Kellie Hammond that put all of his senses on high alert. It had been that way since the moment they'd first met. Of course, then he'd been a brash, cocky twenty-one-year-old, full of himself and his potential success in the racing community. Back then, it had been all about scoring, both on the track and off.

And Kellie Hammond—or Reynolds as she'd been in those days—the innocent seventeen-year-old daughter of the great Jinx Hammond's crew chief, had been a temptation he should have resisted and hadn't. Looking back now, he realized he couldn't.

It shouldn't have happened all those years ago. And it wouldn't have if he hadn't been celebrating his first victory, indulging in too much champagne and fueled by far too much testosterone. He'd spotted her across the room way back then, just as now. She still had that glorious cloud of golden curls tumbling down her back, though the first time he'd seen her, she'd worn it teased into a wild mid-eighties tangle about that stunning face. The memory prompted a smile. She'd also shoveled a few inches worth of makeup onto her face that particular night, which might have accounted for his mistaking her for a full-grown woman instead of a starry-eyed teenager playing dress-up.

Of course, he hadn't recognized her. How could he? Not when her usual uniform around the garages had always been grease-stained jeans, baggy tees that hid that incredible figure and her distinctive hair either braided or stuffed into a ball cap. Cleaned up she'd been irresistible and he hadn't bothered trying.

She was still irresistible. The only question that remained was whether he'd succeed where he'd failed before and hold her at a safe distance, or succumb to his baser instincts. Judging by what had happened two weeks ago in his new HRI office, his chances of success this time around were zero to none.

Worse, Kellie's essence haunted the place, making it almost impossible to closet himself within those four walls and get any work done. Every time he tried, his thoughts strayed to the satin-smooth skin of her cheek and the full ripeness of her mouth, not to mention how close he'd come to yanking her into his arms and kissing her. She was forbidden fruit, now…and then.

"Hey there, Bad."

A heavy hand clapped Lucas on his shoulder and he turned to discover a grinning Cole standing beside him. To anyone looking on, the two appeared the best of friends, unless they were close enough to see the intense dislike glittering in Cole's hazel eyes.

"Whaling," Lucas acknowledged.

Cole shook his head in patent disbelief. "I'm still finding it hard to believe that my biggest rival is now my teammate." He spoke in a carrying voice for the benefit of those nearby, who could overhear their conversation, and his attitude signaled amused camaraderie. "Could have knocked me over with a bulldozer when Kellie made the announcement. I was that surprised."

"Feather."

"Say what?"

"The expression." Lucas spared the other man a brief glance. "You were so surprised you could have been knocked over with a feather."

Whaling's grin broadened. "Ain't nothin' that can

knock me over with a feather." His eyes drifted in Kellie's direction and now he spoke so only Lucas could hear. "Except maybe our boss. Fine lady, that Kellie Hammond."

Something clenched inside Lucas. "I look forward to working with her."

"Unless you win this year's NASCAR Championship. Then all forty-nine percent of her will be working under all fifty-one percent of you. Isn't that how it'll go down?"

The suggestiveness of the taunt had Lucas turning to face Whaling, wanting nothing more than to knock the broad, knowing grin off the other man's face. It was a trademark smile that had charmed the fans and media since Whaling had first hit the circuit, his "golden boy" good looks, twinkling hazel eyes and disarming dimples used to full advantage whether seducing reporters, or the women who'd graced his bed. Did he have plans to seduce Kellie now that Jinx was gone?

Lucas decided to give Whaling the benefit of the doubt, at least for the time being. "I'm sure you didn't mean that to sound the way it did." He returned Cole's smile with one more deadly than charming. "I understand you practice your little quips in front of a mirror. You might want to practice that last one so it doesn't come off wrong in front of the press. That way I won't be forced to make you eat your words on national television."

The "aw, shucks" grin faded, replaced by something far cannier and far more real. "Don't you worry about me and the press," Whaling drawled. "I know exactly what I'm doing there."

"I'm sure you do."

"Boyce!" Leo Farmer, Food Basket's CEO and Lucas's close friend since high school, hailed him from across the room. "Get over here, old man. You're just in time."

Kellie and Jamie stood with Leo, along with Leo's daughter, Stephanie. Lucas frowned. One look warned that his goddaughter was smitten, and it didn't take a rocket scientist to figure out the object of her affections. Jamie Hammond. Based on the shy grin NASCAR's newest driver aimed in her direction, the feeling was mutual. Lucas suppressed a groan. What was it about teenage girls and race car drivers that made them both lose every last brain cell they possessed?

"We're about to unveil the new paint scheme on the Number 56 car," Leo said, clearly oblivious to the swirling undercurrents between the two teenagers. "We've kept the old green and gold colors that Jinx had, but we've given the paint scheme a flashy new look, featuring our logo, of course. I'm really impressed with the final design."

"I can't wait to see it," Lucas said, genuinely pleased for his friend.

"Why don't you get changed," Kellie suggested to Jamie. "They'll want pictures of you with the car."

Jamie reluctantly dragged his attention away from Stephanie. After shaking Leo's hand and giving Stephanie a final grin, he exited the reception hall. Leo and Stephanie headed for the staging area a few minutes later to assist with the presentation, leaving Lucas alone with Kellie.

He could see her guardedness and knew it stemmed from the last time they were alone together. In the two weeks since, they'd both been careful to keep their meetings to only those occasions when others were present to act as a buffer. It had worked, though only to a certain extent. While it prevented new sparks from re-igniting an old flame, the heat smoldered in the background, threatening to erupt at the first opportunity. And they both knew it.

The question that troubled him was whether any of the others around them were aware of the situation. They'd have to be deaf, blind and downright stupid not to sense some of what rippled beneath the surface. And if it were this bad now…how would it be once the season kicked off and they were in each other's company on a more frequent basis?

He released his breath in a silent sigh. He'd deal with that situation when it became too irritating to ignore. In the meantime, he had another problem he needed nipped in the bud. "Those two remind me of old times," he said, inclining his head in the direction Jamie and the Farmers had gone.

Wariness drifted across Kellie's expression, and he could tell she was hastily slapping defenses into place. "Who does? What are you talking about?"

"Jamie and Stephanie."

Her eyes widened in dismay. "You think—" She dismissed the suggestion out of hand. "Don't be ridiculous. They just met."

Aw, hell. She wasn't going to make this easy for him. "You're joking, right?" His laugh held a derisive edge. "We met at a party celebrating my first win and a couple hours later we were in bed together."

"You don't need to remind me," she snapped, rounding on him. "I believe we already covered that ground and agreed to put it behind us. Besides, Jamie's only eighteen."

"Why do I feel compelled to point out that you were barely seventeen, though I didn't know it at the time. I seem to remember you telling me you were twenty."

Twin spots of color rode her cheekbones and her mouth tightened. "I was a child playing at being an adult. I screwed up."

He refused to cut her any slack. "You blindsided me that night, sweetheart. I was definitely at fault since I allowed myself to be seduced by a pretty paint job instead of checking under the hood. But you're guilty of some serious false advertising. Check that. You flat-out lied."

The depth of her hurt caught him off guard. "You're right," she said simply. "I'm sorry."

He shrugged. "On the plus side, you taught me to look beneath the surface, a lesson my ex-wife, Bridgette, reinforced. Now, I expect to get hit, and do my best to protect myself against it." He offered a humorless smile. "I don't trust easily anymore. Makes it simpler all around, don't you think?"

"No, I don't." Her hurt turned to compassion. "If you want the truth, I think it's sad."

"I don't need your pity." He couldn't resist touching her, sliding his calloused hand up the length of her arm to the flimsy strap that clung to her shoulder, holding her gown in place. He traced the edge of the strap and watched as she shivered beneath that single, tantalizing stroke.

"Stop it, Lucas."

He ignored her. Instead, he shifted closer, taking a perverse pleasure in the intensity of the reaction that rippled back and forth between them. "Listen up, partner," he murmured. "Stephanie's my goddaughter and I'm not about to let Jamie hurt her. She's the innocent in all this, ready, willing and able to be blind-sided by a randy teenaged stock car driver. No matter what it takes, history will not repeat itself."

"You're overreacting," she protested.

"This isn't open to negotiation. This isn't a 49/51 give-and-take. Not on this issue. This is me warning you that if someone gets hurt, it won't be Stephanie. Are we clear?"

Her chin swept upward and she met his gaze with a defiance at distinct odds with her words. "I'll speak to Jamie."

"Wise decision." He leaned forward, crowding her in the hopes it would drive home his point. "And when you speak to him, you might want to remind him that Food Basket is paying for his ride this year. That ride won't last long if he messes with the owner's daughter."

She didn't back down. Nor did she allow his physical presence to intimidate her, despite the sexual awareness that flowed with such reckless abandon. "I can handle my son," she retorted in a fierce, taut voice. "You said your piece, now back off."

"Fair enough." He shifted to one side, though not as far away as he suspected she'd have liked. "How's he holding up?" he asked, deliberately changing the subject.

"Fine." She bit off the word, refusing to let go of her anger. "He's just fine."

"Don't go getting defensive again. He's an eighteen-year-old kid who's been thrown into the big leagues. That can't be easy." He tilted his head to one side. "Just out of curiosity, why didn't you start him off in the NASCAR Busch Series?"

"It was Jinx's decision." Her anger lessened, pride taking its place. "And Jamie's good. Very good."

"A few years' seasoning wouldn't have hurt. If anything, it would have given him more confidence and a chance to hone his craft. You've thrown him in the deep end and he could very well drown. Dead in the water stays dead in the water. You don't recover from that."

"You're not saying anything I haven't already considered," she surprised him by admitting. "But Jinx was adamant. Even my dad backed him."

"Darrell supported Jinx's decision?" Lucas asked in surprise.

"All the way. He said that in all his years in the business, he's only seen one other driver with as much talent as Jamie."

"And who was that?"

The change that came over her surprised him. She stiffened and took a quick step back. "I—I don't remember."

"Liar." He regarded her with lazy amusement. "Come on, spill. Who was it? Jinx?"

"No."

His mouth compressed. "Tell me it wasn't Whaling."

"Not him." She met his gaze and he saw the answer in the haunting blue of her eyes, saw it even before she told him. "It was you, Lucas."

Feedback from a microphone screeched, preventing the need for a response. Just as well, since her comment had swept every thought from his head. He forced himself to focus on the dais. Leo and Stephanie stood on the curtained platform and waited for the excited chatter to fade.

"Welcome, folks," Leo said. "We'd like to say how delighted we are to be a part of the NASCAR NEXTEL Cup Series family. And we're downright thrilled to be sponsoring one of the hottest, most exciting new drivers to hit the circuit in many a year. Please welcome back the legendary Number 56 car, driven by Jamie 'Jinx Junior' Hammond."

"Oh, God," Kellie whispered.

Lucas doubted she was even aware that she'd clutched his arm. "What's wrong?" he asked.

"I wish Leo hadn't called Jamie that."

Lucas shook his head. "I don't get it. What's the problem? Doesn't he like being compared to his old man?"

"He loves the idea of having inherited Jinx's skill."
Damn. "It's being another jinx that has him worried."

"Yes."

The curtain parted and Jamie stood there in his uniform beside the redesigned car. The bright green and gold gleamed beneath the overhead lights, showcasing Food Basket's colors and logo. Jamie was grinning, but Lucas sensed a level of nervousness beneath the brash smile. Normal, given the circumstances. But he suspected Kellie was right. What kid in Jamie's position wouldn't worry about having inherited the family curse? It would be a tough legacy to overcome, especially if the press decided they liked the handle "Jinx Junior." And as catchy as it was, he suspected the media would be all over it.

"He's going to have to come to terms with it sooner or later," Lucas said. "Everyone has bad luck. There's not a driver out there who hasn't wrecked on one occasion or another."

Kellie gave an impatient nod. "I don't disagree with that." A frown of concern creased her brow. "The question is...can Jamie accept those incidents as part of the sport? Or is he going to blame it on the family jinx?"

CHAPTER FOUR

"WELL, FOLKS, it's finally here. The Sunday you've all been waiting for. In just a few short hours the NASCAR NEXTEL Cup Series season will start with a roar heard 'round the world as forty-three drivers vie for stock car racing's most prized reward—a win at Daytona.

"This is the most prestigious race of the NASCAR season. A win here is the most sought after of all the tracks in the circuit. Despite being a restrictor plate race, speeds nearing 180 miles per hour and the infamous 'bump drafting' almost guarantee there being unavoidable contact at some point during the race. The main question is...who will get caught up in the inevitable collisions and who will bump his way to the front and take the first checkered flag of the season?

"The answer to all those questions is just a few hours away."

"ARE YOU NERVOUS?" Stephanie asked.

Jamie shrugged, not ready to admit that his stomach was so knotted up that he wasn't sure he'd keep his breakfast down. "I'm mostly excited."

"We are, too." She gazed up at him with huge, chocolate-brown eyes, eyes that reflected an unmistakable adoration. "Everyone at Food Basket's rooting for you. We have signs up everywhere and cutout posters, too. We're all wearing your colors. I've never seen so much green and gold in my life."

"Wow." Now he was sure he'd be sick. "I'll…I'll do my best not to let everyone down."

"Don't be silly. You won't let anyone down."

She caught her bottom lip between her teeth and all of a sudden he didn't feel quite as sick. What would she do if he asked her for a kiss for good luck? What would she do if he caught that pretty little lip between his own teeth? Maybe if he won the race she'd let him.

An image blossomed to life in his head, of him standing in Victory Lane while confetti filled the air and champagne soaked his uniform. He'd stand in the door frame of his car and leap on top of his team. And then they'd poke a microphone in his face and ask how it felt to be just eighteen years old, win his first race ever and have that first win be at Daytona—an unheard-of feat. He'd laugh, full of confidence and pumped beyond belief at the win.

"Guess this means you can't call me Jinx Junior anymore," he'd tell the world.

Then he'd turn to Stephanie and he'd sweep her into his arms. And he'd kiss that beautiful mouth while everyone cheered. Best of all, she'd kiss him back.

"Jamie?" She wasn't gazing at him adoringly anymore, but with something more like concern. "Are you okay?"

"What?" The dream faded. "Oh, sure. I'm great."

"You *are* worried, aren't you?" A tiny frown pulled her brows together for an instant before a broad smile lit up her face. "I have an idea."

A kiss for luck? he almost said. "Something for good luck?" he asked instead.

"Exactly." Before he could drag her into his arms and claim his kiss, she pulled off the locket she wore around her neck and slipped it over his head. "Here," she said, tucking it beneath his T-shirt. "This belonged to my mother. I haven't taken it off since she died...until now."

"Oh, man. Are you sure?"

Her smile was the most beautiful he'd ever seen. "Positive. See if it doesn't help. Whenever you get nervous, you'll know I'm right there with you, cheering you on."

Okay, it wasn't a kiss. But it wasn't bad. A girl as beautiful as Stephanie giving him her most prized possession as a good luck charm? "Thanks. This is—"

Before he could get the words out, she lifted up onto her toes and feathered a swift kiss across his mouth. "And that's for luck, too," she said, hot pink sweeping across her cheekbones.

He couldn't have asked for a better send-off. Filled with sudden confidence, he leaned down and dared to steal a second kiss. "I'll see you in Victory Lane," he said.

KELLIE RAN THROUGH a final check of her notes as the pre-race meeting started to break up. The three drivers and their crew chiefs had congregated in the plush conference room that took up the entire front section of Lucas's Wolf Sportsman hauler. As last year's NASCAR NEXTEL Cup Championship winner, he had the garage closest to pit road, as well as the number one spot for his hauler, a convenience she intended to take full advantage of.

Lucas stood talking to his crew chief, Dipstick, a tall, heavyset man with eyes that possessed a permanent twinkle of humor and what most in the business called "the best mechanic's hands" in racing. Jamie stood on the fringes, watching avidly, absorbing everything.

"Did you find out what was wrong with the engine?" she asked Dipstick, glancing up from her notes.

"Broken camshaft."

She frowned in concern. "Do we have to worry about Cole or Jamie having a similar problem during the race?"

"Not at all. It's not an engine defect, just one bad part. Since we brought the camshaft with us when we moved over to HRI, it shouldn't affect your other two drivers."

"I'll start at the back of the field because of the engine change, of course," Lucas added. "But since Jamie's back there, the two of us can hook up and work our way to the front."

No one had actually said it, but they all knew that Jamie had been lucky to make the race at all. Since he hadn't participated in the series last year, he'd had to qualify his way into the field by being one of the fastest of the cars not guaranteed a spot in the race.

"I'm not all that far ahead of Jamie," Cole said, joining in the conversation. "I'll watch out for the kid."

"Really?" Jamie glanced from one driver to the other. "You'd both draft with me?"

Cole stepped to Jamie's side and dropped a companionable hand on the boy's shoulder. "Why not? It'll give me an opportunity to knock some of that rookie shine off you." He offered the boy one of his patented smiles. "But once we get toward the front, it's up to you to stay with me."

Jamie made a visible effort to maintain a professional demeanor, but a hint of boyish excitement slipped through. "I'll do my best."

"I'm sure you will."

Jamie turned to Lucas. "You'll draft with me, too?"

"No bump drafting going into the corners," he said. "I know you've seen some of the wrecks that happen here when an overly enthusiastic driver's too aggressive with his bumper. Not a bad strategy on the straightaway, but going into the corner, it's a disaster waiting to happen." He spared Cole a brief glance. "If the three of us team up, we should be able to get to the front within a couple dozen laps. That way we can all pit together should the race stay green, so we don't lose the draft."

"Last ten laps, it's every man for himself," Cole added with a broad grin. "This is one race I intend to win."

"Agreed."

Jamie's eyes shone. "Thanks, guys. I really appreciate it."

Kellie suppressed a smile and buried her head in her notes. When she looked up again it was to discover that, with the exception of Lucas, the place had cleared out. Sudden awareness swept over her like a tidal wave, and the urge to compensate for the unwanted sexual tension made her more formal than she'd have been otherwise.

"Sorry. I was so caught up in work, I didn't realize everyone had left." She stood, straightening her notes and attaching them to her clipboard. "I'll get out of your way."

"You're fine. No hurry." He continued to study her with a keenness that prompted an instinctive wariness.

"What is it, Lucas?"

"How did your talk with Jamie go?"

She didn't need to ask which talk. He could only mean the one she'd promised to have regarding Stephanie. "Uncomfortable for both of us," she replied. "But I said what needed to be said."

"I'm not sure how that's possible, considering they're dating."

Kellie tossed her clipboard onto the table. "Stephanie has a father, Lucas. I've spoken to him about the situation. We've established reasonable ground rules for the two of them, though there's only so much we can do considering they're both eighteen." She rubbed at the tension headache forming at her temples. "I can promise you one thing. They're not going to get into the same predicament we did."

"Or that you and Jinx did?" He eyed her curiously. "Does Jamie know?"

"He knows I was pregnant when Jinx and I married. He's also enough of a math whiz to subtract his age from mine and come up with 'too damn young' when figuring out how old I was when I had him. Not to mention the lecture he's heard at least a dozen times about combining teenage hormones with massive stupidity. Trust me, he gets the message."

"You can't afford to lose Food Basket as a sponsor."

She glared at him. "Credit me with some common sense. I do know that." She fought for patience with only limited success. "I'm giving you some latitude here because, like it or not, you're my partner and deserve to be in the loop. But this situation isn't any of your business. It's personal." She made a point of emphasizing that final word, not that it made much impact.

"Everything that affects HRI is my business," he corrected. "Especially something that might cause trouble for one of my oldest friends or have an adverse financial impact on a company I've paid a pretty penny to purchase."

"Wait a minute." Her frown deepened. "Do you think I'd do something underhanded to harm HRI or diminish its value, just to hit out at you?"

"Not if it meant hurting Jamie."

"Only if it meant hurting you." It wasn't a question. "You tell me."

She knew he had a low opinion of her based on their past, but it never occurred to her it was this bad. Anger battled with distress. "I wouldn't do that to you, Lucas. I wouldn't do that to anyone." She needed to have her say and didn't care whether or not he believed her. "I know you don't trust me. Not after what happened between us all those years ago. That you think I'm…I don't know…a gold digger or something. But I'm not and I never was. I'm also aware that nothing I can say will change your opinion. I'm just hoping that over time, you'll get to know the person I've become instead of the irresponsible child you remember."

He actually considered her words, before nodding. "Seems fair."

"Good." She picked up her clipboard again. "Because here's the other side of that coin. I don't give a damn whether you approve of me or even like me. All we have to do is work together. Got it?"

"Oh, I've got it." He came for her. In the confined space of the hauler's conference room, it only took a few steps to reach her. With one quick tug, he had her tumbling into his arms. "There's just one minor correction. You may wish it's all business between us. Hell, I know I do. But there's one small problem that keeps getting in our way."

The clipboard clattered to the floor. "What?"

"This."

He molded her against him, the fit sheer perfection. She slipped between his thighs as though she'd been shaped for just that purpose, their bodies aligning curve to angle. There was something about the feel of a man's body—the lean hardness, the tempered strength—that awoke an awareness of her own femininity and intensified it. It had been so long since she'd been held like this. Been kissed with a man's passion rather than the chaste sweetness of a friend. She needed this. Needed it more than she'd realized.

He gathered her up, focusing on her to the exclusion of all else. A shudder of longing trembled through her. This was wrong. So wrong on so many levels. But right now, she didn't care. She'd willingly pay whatever price fate decreed for this brief indiscretion, if it meant having a taste of the forbidden one more time.

Slowly, so slowly she could have screamed in frustration, he lowered his head. His mouth brushed hers. A sampling, teasing and incomplete. Then another one, as though testing the suppleness of her mouth and figuring out the best possible way to join their lips. She knew he'd come for her now, sink deep and long. That this final kiss would be the one she'd waited nearly nineteen years to experience again.

She actually swore when someone hammered on the door of the conference room, a single bitter punctuation to the interruption. Without a word, Lucas released her and stepped back. Somehow he managed to recover his equilibrium in those few seconds while she was still caught in the backwash of emotional turmoil. In one smooth move, he swept up her clipboard and handed it to her.

"To be continued," he murmured.

And just like that, he opened the door to business, while closing and locking it on everything else, leaving Kellie more off balance than she'd been in nearly two decades.

THE FLAG DROPPED at precisely four in the afternoon and the field drove straight toward the fading sun.

The level of noise never failed to astonish Kellie as it echoed across pit lane. Lifting her binoculars, she watched as her three cars flashed across the start/finish line. Cole in his distinctive blue-and-silver Perfection Tools car hugged the bottom lane and zipped by. Farther back she found her son in his green-and-gold Food Basket, maintaining his position on the outside lane. And finally, Lucas's shiny black car with its distinctive bright red flames brought up the back of the pack.

She remained on her feet for the first few laps around the two-and-a-half-mile track, the same as the crowd, checking the monitor on the war wagon when the cars moved out of view around Turn One. On the fifth lap, as they headed toward the front stretch, approaching 180 miles per hour, the car directly in front of Cole lost control and spun.

Kellie gripped the railing and watched the crash unfold. The wrecking car pirouetted in a graceful 360, sending up a billowing cloud of brake smoke. She could tell Cole was standing on his brakes, holding his line as he waited for the spinning car to slide into the infield grass or up the track. It went up, clipping the wall and then ricocheting across the track into oncoming traffic.

All around Cole, cars were wrecking in chain reaction to the braking ahead of them or because they caught a piece of the various accidents. She watched anxiously for Jamie and Lucas. Jamie appeared out of the smoke, swerving to hit pit lane to avoid the wreck. Lucas was right on his bumper. They darted past their pit boxes and back onto the track, blending in with the other drivers who'd slowed behind the pace car.

After nearly twenty years in the business, she would have thought she'd get used to the wrecks and to waiting to see whether her driver was involved. But it never ceased to get her heart racing, sending the nerve-wracking adrenaline crashing through her system. She worked to keep it from showing, switching from one driver's frequency to the next and listening in on their comments through their headphones.

Her son was talking excitedly to his crew chief, Lucky, and to Paps. If her adrenaline was skyrocketing, her son's was in orbit. She smiled, listening as her dad calmed him with a story about one of Jinx's near misses. Then Lucky took over, discussing how the pit stop would go. She caught the tail end of the same discussion between Lucas and his crew chief, Dipstick.

Cole was busy giving a blow-by-blow description of the wreck, his voice calm and droll. "Oh, and the right front's going down. Must have caught a piece of the debris."

"Slow 'er down. Don't want to knock the fenders off," his crew chief, R.J., replied. "We're going with four new and a round of left rear wedge to tighten you up."

The pit stops went smoothly, each driver hitting their marks perfectly. To her delight, Lucas and Jamie came out together, the Number 121 car nipping right in front of her son's Number 56. He'd learn a lot if the two could draft together, because he'd been correct in his assessment at their pre-race meeting. Not many drivers trusted an inexperienced rookie enough to draft with him. Not at Daytona. This was the big leagues and Jamie hadn't proven himself, yet.

The race restarted, this time without incident, and the miles began to pile up. Midway through the five-hundred-mile race, all three of her drivers hooked up, with Cole in the lead. The timing couldn't have been better since they were coming up on green flag stops. This would be a true test of Jamie's skill and ability, she knew.

And yet when she focused her binoculars on her team cars, for some reason it was Lucas's car that filled the lenses.

"OKAY, JAMIE, just follow your teammates and match your speed to theirs. We can't afford a speeding penalty. You got it?"

"Sure thing, Lucky."

"Now, because of how we qualified, your box is ahead of the others. You'll be peeling off first. I'll count you down and you stop in the center rear of the box, just like we practiced. Careful you're not outside the box and we want extra space in front in case Carl pits at the same time we do. He's right in front of us. Understand?"

"We're hitting pit road right now."

"I've got you, Jamie. In five. Four. Three. Two. And stop."

His pit team leapt into action, scurrying around to his right side. The car jacked upward and he heard the air gun shrieking above the throaty idling of his engine. An extension pole dropped, swiping at his grill. And then his team jumped up and pelted around to the left side of his car. Jamie revved his engine, preparing to leave the instant the jackman dropped the jack, which would be his signal to go. The seconds ticked by.

"Lucky?"

"Hold it! Hold it! Don't go, Jamie. We've got a lugnut hung up."

Tension tied his stomach in knots. *Please, don't let me be jinxed like my father.* "Hurry up," he urged. "I'll lose the draft. They're going to leave without me."

"You're clear. Go, go, go!"

He smoked the wheels, fishtailing the car as he left the pits. "Watch your speed, son," he heard Paps warn. Jamie checked his RPMs and swore. He eased up on the gas, praying he hadn't gone far enough over pit road speed to incur a penalty.

"Listen to me, Jamie." The sound of his crew chief's voice came through his headset. His voice was so calm. Soothing. And he found himself instantly relaxing. "You've missed the draft with Cole and Lucas. Don't worry about it. There's still a lot of race left and plenty of time to catch them again. You have two other drivers coming off pit road with you. I'm going to talk to their people and let them know you'll be the caboose on their train. Just stay directly behind them and follow where they lead. Don't try to pass in order to catch up with Cole and Lucas. Got it?"

"No problem."

But it was a problem, and the race went downhill from there. No matter what he did, or how hard he tried, he couldn't seem to get ahead. Every time he hooked up with a pack of cars, he'd get booted out of line and lose the draft.

"Patience, Jamie," Paps would reassure him. "This isn't Saturday night dirt tracking. You have to pace yourself."

And that would be fine, if it weren't for the close calls. They came from every direction, without pause. Cars that ran up on his rear bumper and got him loose. Cars that edged within inches of his door, so close he could have shook hands with the other driver. Cars that slid into a gap in front of him where only half a car would fit.

On top of all that, the speeds were incredible and took every ounce of focus he possessed. If he dared take a hand off the steering wheel, he'd have felt for Stephanie's locket. But he didn't dare, not as daylight faded and darkness crept over the track. He adjusted his grip on the steering wheel, amazed at how different Daytona looked under the lights. If he didn't know better, he'd think it a different venue altogether.

In the final quarter of the race, he took a chance and slipped into the middle of a pack of cars moving forward and managed to drive to within sight of Cole's 199. Just a few more laps and he'd be able to drop in behind and help push his teammate toward the front. Once they made it into the lead pack, he and Cole could battle it out to the finish line.

Jamie shifted ever so slightly in his seat, just enough to feel the press of Stephanie's locket through his uniform. The image of her in his arms in the middle of Victory Lane flashed through his mind again—the vision so real, he could practically taste the sweetness of her kiss, smell the champagne and see the whirlwind of confetti filling the air. The shouts and cheers would deafen him and the press would all be jockeying for an interview. His mom would be there, beaming in pride. And Cole and Lucas would run up, whomping him around the back and shoulders as they congratulated him. He'd grin at them, knowing that he fit in. He was one of them. He was an honest-to-goodness NASCAR NEXTEL Cup Series regular and deserved to be there, even at the unheard-of age of eighteen.

The bump came from behind, sudden and wrenching, catching him at his most vulnerable, when he'd foolishly allowed his attention to waver from the task at hand. It was a critical error with disastrous results.

It all happened in a split second. Jamie tightened his grip on the steering wheel, struggling to catch the car, but his distraction proved to be a major mistake. The car darted toward the wall so fast it was little more than a blur. He vaguely heard Paps in his ear, issuing a sharp warning right before he hit.

Slamming the wall at 178 miles per hour hurt worse than anything he'd ever felt before, knocking the breath clean out of him and jarring every bone in his body. He rebounded off the wall and shot straight toward a pack of cars riding low on the track. He had time for one brief thought…he was going to hit them, and hit hard. And then he did.

Stock cars ricocheted like billiard balls, brilliant splashes of twisted metal spinning in clouds of smoke across the forty-foot width of track and onto the apron before hitting the grass that separated the front stretch from the pits. All Jamie could do was hang on and brace himself as the car began to roll.

CHAPTER FIVE

KELLIE WATCHED in horror as the front valence of the Number 56 car dug into the grass along the front stretch. Her son's car went airborne. It landed square on its tailpipe, twirled in a perfect spiral before cartwheeling end over end. Twice. Three times. Four. After the fifth flip, it crashed down on its lid and skidded for what seemed like an eternity before coming to rest at the exit to pit road.

Kellie knew she was shrieking Jamie's name, though no sound escaped the knot that held her throat closed. She could hear her father's voice booming in her ear.

"Jamie?" It amazed her that he could maintain such utter calm. "Talk to me, boy."

Silence.

"Son? Are you injured?"

Silence.

Darrell keyed the mike once more. "Come on now. How about reassuring your poor old mother before she suffers a conniption? You okay, or should I start panicking, too?"

There was a second's worth of static, and then, "'Kay. I'm okay."

Jamie sounded groggy. He had to have taken a hard, hard hit. And with all those flips, his head was probably still spinning. Kellie forced herself not to consider the worst.

"Give me a status report, Jamie," Lucky ordered crisply.

"Car's a bit wrecked."

Tears of relief welled into her eyes.

"Yeah, we sort of figured that. How about you?"

"Oh, hanging in there. Upside down, as a matter of fact. As for injuries…" There was another momentary silence. "Everything seems to be where it's supposed to be. Everything moves that's supposed to move. Maybe even a few things that shouldn't."

"What things?" Darrell asked sharply.

"Kidding. I'm kidding. Lighten up."

"Jamie. You're hanging upside down in a wrecked car. We'll lighten up, but it won't be any time soon," Lucky said.

Darrell's gruff laugh sliced through Kellie's headphones. "Christmas would be a good bet."

The emergency vehicles raced up to Jamie's race car and the EMTs hopped out, bellying into the grass so they could unhook the trapped driver. Five minutes later, they had him freed from the wreck.

"WELL, FOLKS, the biggest crash of the race has just happened and it was one of the most serious we've seen at Daytona in many a year. The thirteen-car pileup occurred on lap 160 of 200, precipitated when young Jinx

Junior was bumped from behind by fellow rookie, Davy Ellis, who sent the Number 56 car careening into the front stretch wall.

"As if that weren't enough, Jinx Junior then shot down in front of the field of oncoming cars before he hit the grass and flipped end over end a staggering five times. Fans were on their feet cheering this intrepid young driver when he crawled out of his wreck. As of yet, we have no official word on his condition. Stay tuned for more information...."

CHECKING THE TV screen on the console in Lucky's war wagon, Kellie watched as the emergency crew helped brace Jamie as he stood. It appeared to her as though his legs weren't quite solid beneath him. After taking a minute to catch his breath, he got his knees locked in place. Unfastening his helmet, he yanked it off.

Cheers erupted around him, and the camera tightened its angle, revealing the momentary confusion that swept across his face. It also showed the instant he realized that the cheers were directed his way, surprise widening his blue eyes. He lifted his arm in a tentative wave and the volume increased dramatically. That elicited a broad grin, and he gave the crowd a thumbs-up. A minute later he was ushered into the waiting ambulance and whisked away.

"I'm going to the care center," Kellie informed Jamie's crew chief, Lucky, as she tore off her headphones. "Let me know how Lucas and Cole finish."

"Will do."

By the time she arrived at the infield care center, the

doctor had completed his examination and stepped out of the room to consult with her. "Aside from a few bruises, he's come through the accident in amazing shape," she was informed. "But we're going to play it safe. We're about to have him transported to the hospital for some scans. I assume you want to go with him?"

Kellie nodded and closed her eyes in a brief prayer of gratitude. She could feel the reaction settling in as the initial shock of adrenaline subsided, causing her to tremble uncontrollably. She could have lost him. She could have lost her son. He could have ended up in a wheelchair like Jinx. He could have had bones broken, broken beyond repair. A thousand worst-case scenarios whipped through her mind, each more hideous than the one before, the brutal images lashing at her deepest vulnerability.

She steeled herself against the onslaught of fear, fighting back for all she was worth. She'd been in this business a long time. True, she'd seen injuries, but they were few and far between. NASCAR had worked miracles providing for safer racing conditions, from head restraints to softer walls to roof flaps, as well as carbon fiber seats. Every last one of those improvements had done their job and protected her son. Now it was time to do her job.

She took several deep breaths and forced a smile to her mouth. She could do this. Sure, she could. From the time Jamie had first set eyes on a race car when he'd been little more than a toddler, he'd been hooked on the sport, working with the sort of focus and dedication that bred champions. She'd seen that light in his eyes, that light she'd seen in countless drivers over the years. It was as though the stock cars called to them on some subconscious level, weaving a siren's song around their heart and mind and soul.

Jamie had been born to do this. And based on the amount of talent he'd demonstrated to date, he was going to be part of this business for a long time to come. She could either accept that, or allow her fears to gain the upper hand, to control her every thought and drive all her decisions. Once she started down that path, she'd lose her way in some mighty prickly brambles. She'd never be the same again, and she flat-out wouldn't allow that to happen. Time to suck it up and deal with this by setting the right tone for this and all similar incidents in the future. Clamping her back teeth together, she opened the door to the examination room and joined her son.

"Hey, there, you," she greeted him with a teasing grin. "Just wanted you to know that the judges gave you a 9.9 on your stellar routine out there. It would have been a solid ten, but they deducted a tenth for that slide after you landed."

IT TOOK A FULL HOUR after the race before Lucas managed to hitch a ride to the hospital and he was chomping at the bit to see for himself that the kid hadn't damaged himself too badly. Darrell had gotten there fifteen minutes earlier, and he and Kellie were in Jamie's room where the youngster was being held overnight for observation. Lucas paused in the doorway, smiling at the familial camaraderie the three exhibited.

"You held your own out there, son. Good job," Darrell was telling his grandson.

"Before the crash, or after?" Jamie asked wryly.

"Both. You ran a good race, right up until you lost your focus."

Jamie's gaze jerked up to meet his grandfather's. "How did you—"

"How did I know? You're joking, right?"

Hot color streaked across Jamie's cheekbones. "Sorry, Paps. Stupid question."

"Don't be sorry. Just don't do it again. I don't know where your head went. But you better make sure it doesn't go there again." He clapped a hand on Jamie's shoulder. "You handled yourself like a pro when you climbed out of that car. And you probably earned yourself some sympathy fans."

That didn't seem to make him feel any better. "To be honest, I'd rather earn a few fans who like the way I race," Jamie said, "rather than earn fans who like the way I crash."

"Get a few more races under your belt and you will."

"Hey, Bad." Jamie brightened as he noticed Lucas for the first time. He leaned forward with undisguised eagerness. "How'd you finish?"

"Fifth."

"All right!" Jamie held up his hand for a high five. "How'd Cole do?"

"Nicked me by one."

"Man, I wish I could have been there to see it." He grinned. "Even better, I wish I could have been there and done it with you."

"You will. Next time."

Lucas spared Kellie a quick glance. Though she appeared relaxed, he could see the lingering echoes of distress in the tightness around her mouth and the weariness darkening her eyes. It wasn't an auspicious start to the season and he couldn't help but wonder how she'd handle an entire year of this sort of ongoing pressure. If she thought dealing with Jamie's racing career would be similar to what she'd experienced in the past with Jinx and Cole, she'd just discovered differently, in the most unpleasant fashion possible. He could only hope that Jamie didn't make a habit of crashing. He wasn't sure Kellie could handle the strain.

The next hour whipped by and Lucas lingered, enjoying the give-and-take as the four of them conducted a lap-by-lap analysis of the race. After he'd assured himself that his youngest teammate had come through his wreck in reasonable shape, both physically and mentally, he stood to leave. Kellie followed him out the door.

"Thank you," she said in an undertone. "He needed that."

"The wreck wasn't his fault." Lucas shrugged. "Or not completely. Ellis hit him when Jamie was heading into the corner. If he were a little more experienced or a bit more focused, he might have been able to hang on to his car. But even an experienced driver would have had trouble avoiding the wall after taking the shot he did."

"I haven't seen the replay," she admitted. "But that was my impression when I saw it unfolding."

"It wasn't the greatest career start. But it was far from the worst. Not all the errors were his." He dropped a hand on her shoulder and studied her upturned face. The hint of tension he'd noted earlier was more apparent now. "You're going to have to find a way of separating your emotions from your job or you're going to burn out before Bristol."

She opened her mouth to argue, then lifted a shoulder in grudging acceptance of the truth. "I know." To his dismay, tears pricked her eyes, though she managed to smile through them. "It was my first race, too. Give me time. I'll do better."

"It was a nasty wreck. Anyone would have had a rough time dealing with it."

"Thanks for understanding." And then she covered her face with her hands and burst into tears.

Without a word, Lucas maneuvered her down the corridor before Jamie caught wind of his mother's distress. Pulling her into his arms, he simply held her until the storm passed. It didn't take her long to recover. He had the distinct impression that she wasn't the crying sort. No doubt she saw it as a weakness.

"I'm sorry," she said, looking everywhere but at him.

"No problem." He cupped her face and forced her to meet his eyes. "He's going to be all right."

Her chin trembled. "I just keep thinking—"

"There's your first mistake. No thinking. And maybe this will help." He lowered his head until their mouths were a mere whisper apart. "I seem to remember our getting interrupted earlier. I think this might be an excellent time to finish what we started."

He didn't sample her lips this time. There were no teasing preliminaries. Instead, he kissed her with a sweeping demand that took them both from zero to one eighty in three seconds flat. He heard that tiny moan again, a moan that had haunted his dreams. A moan that spoke of sultry nights of endless lovemaking. It drove him to deepen the kiss, slipping between her lips to find the honeyed sweetness within.

She tasted amazing. He had faded recollections of how good, but they were mere shadows of the real thing. How could he have forgotten? How could he have dismissed something this unique? The callowness of youth, no doubt. Well, he wouldn't make that mistake again. This time he'd brand the next few moments on both of their memories.

He turned, maneuvering her the few steps it took until her back hit the wall. He wasn't sure they'd be able to stand, otherwise. He filled his arms with her, every soft rounded inch. He wanted to explore it all. He wanted to put his stamp on her, one that she'd never forget, anymore than he'd been able to forget her.

She pulled away ever so slightly. "We need to stop." Her tongue crept out to probe the swollen contours of her mouth. "This is wrong."

He regarded her with lazy amusement. "Wrong that we kissed? Or wrong because we're in a public place?"

"Either. Both." The breath shuddered from her lungs. "Jinx has only been gone a few months."

"He wouldn't have wanted you to stop living."

"That doesn't mean…" He caught the hint of despair in her words. "That doesn't excuse what I'm doing."

"It's just a kiss, meant to comfort and distract." He smiled down at her, his thumbs tracing the bold sweep of her cheekbones. "Did it work?"

She relaxed into his hold and returned his smile. "What do you think?"

"You do look distracted. As for comforted…" He tilted his head to one side to assess. "Hmm."

"Not there?"

"Close." He lowered his head. "But definitely not there."

COLE STOOD AT THE END of the hospital corridor and stared at the embracing couple. His hands clenched into fists and the cocky pleasure he'd felt at edging Boyce out of his way to finish a nose ahead was swallowed in a white-hot rage.

Boyce. Again.

It was always Boyce. He'd stolen the NASCAR Championship last year on the last lap of the last race. Somehow he'd gotten the press to consider him HRI's "premier" driver. And now, when Kellie was finally available, he'd swept in and taken her, as well.

Cole shook his head. No. No way would he let that happen. In all the years he'd been with Hammond

Racing, he'd never once made a move on Kellie. He'd had too much respect for Jinx. He'd also known how that sort of mistake guaranteed a career implosion. As inconvenient as it was on occasion, he'd always been careful to ensure that his southern hemisphere never outraced his northern. But from the minute Jinx had been diagnosed with cancer, Cole had marked Kellie as his.

And no one was going to take that away from him. He'd worked too long and too hard not to reap the ultimate benefits—a starring position in Kellie's life and in HRI's corporate hierarchy.

He watched as the kiss finally ended and the two drew apart. She'd been crying, he noted. No doubt over Jamie. Understandable, all things considered. The kid had taken a bad hit.

Maybe if he'd gotten here a few minutes sooner instead of pushing for extra airtime, he could have been the one to comfort her. Maybe he'd have been the one kissing Kellie right now. Well, one thing was an absolute certainty. He might not have been the first to get his hands on the delectable Mrs. Hammond. But he'd sure as hell be the last.

JAMIE EXITED the hospital. His mother had promised to meet him, but instead he was stunned to find a crowd of reporters and camera crew waiting for him.

"Was it the Hammond Jinx?" one reporter asked, shoving a microphone in his face. "Has it been passed from father to son?"

The pack surrounded him, pressing in. "Are you going to be looking for payback against Davy Ellis when you get to Fontana?"

"Were you hurt, Jamie? Are you okay?"

"Are you at all concerned about making it into next week's race without any driver points to secure you a starting spot?"

"Jamie, did your parents make a mistake? Should they have started you off in the NASCAR Busch Series first? Are you too inexperienced to be racing in the NASCAR NEXTEL Cup?"

The questions bombarded him and he knew he must look foolish standing there gaping at them all. Finally, his brain kicked in and he offered a wide grin, hoping it didn't look as phony as it felt. "First, I'm just fine. I've had worse bumps and bruises playing with my dog. Second, I'd like to thank the best team sponsor out there yesterday, Food Basket. I'd also like to thank my outstanding team. We're still knocking out a few of the kinks, but you'll see a big improvement next week."

"Will there be payback for Davy having bumped you?"

Were they kidding? "You know that's part of racing. Davy's a great guy. He was just trying to do a bit of bump drafting. Guess we were too close to the corner for it to work."

Another reporter sidled in. "Was it your inexperience that caused the wreck?"

Jamie swallowed, struggling to find an answer that was honest, while remaining politic. "Experience can only help me become a better driver. I wish this race could have ended under better circumstances. But I wouldn't be here if HRI didn't feel I deserved to be." He held up his hands at the flood of responses. "Granted, my parents started the company. But they've been in the business a long time. If my dad hadn't felt I was ready, he'd never have agreed to put me in the Number 56 car. In case you never noticed, he was sort of protective of that number. I'm just sorry he wasn't there for my first race."

"Do you think your father would have been disappointed in your performance?"

He tried to keep from flinching at the question, hoping he hadn't just given them more ammunition to use against him. "Come on, guys. Give me a chance." He smiled with as much good humor as he could summon, but some of the comments had hit hard, scraping along a few of his deepest held insecurities. "See what I do next week before writing me off, okay?"

The questions continued, questions Jamie answered as diplomatically as possible. But a part of him remained detached from the proceedings, a part that couldn't help but wonder if they were right. Had he been started too soon? Would his father have been disappointed or had second thoughts about his son's talent? Granted he'd had unbelievable success in all of the other venues he'd ever attempted, garnering championships in every single arena he'd raced in to date. But that didn't guarantee the same sort of success here and now, in one of the most competitive motor sports out there.

One question above all others worried him the most. Had he inherited the Hammond Jinx? He didn't believe in such things. At least, he'd tried not to. But this wasn't the best start to his racing career. And he couldn't help but wonder...what sort of luck would next week bring?

Cole Whaling approached just then and threw a companionable arm around him. He deflected the rest of the reporters' questions, easing the moment with his usual humorous quips and droll comments.

"How you feeling, kid?" Cole asked, once the reporters had left and they were alone.

"Bruised and battered," Jamie muttered. "And not just from the wreck."

"Ah. Your first run-in with the press. Yeah, that can get dicey if you're not careful. Tell you what. Why don't we go out and do some medicinal healing. I'll even give you some pointers on how to handle the press. What do you say?"

"I don't know." He scanned the approaching cars. "Mom said she was coming to pick me up."

"I offered to come and get you. She's got a lot on her plate right now considering we're out in California next weekend. I thought picking you up might make things easier for her."

"Really?" Jamie asked, secretly impressed. The offer made him feel like a "real" stock car driver. One of the guys. "I wouldn't object to a bit of medicinal healing. But I'm only eighteen, so..."

"I'm not talking about alcohol. I know better than

that." He winked. "But there's plenty of other hell we can raise that'll do the job almost as well. You up for it?"

Was he kidding? "Do your worst."

CHAPTER SIX

"SHOCKING NEWS OUT of the HRI camp. Police were called in the early hours of the morning to respond to an incident involving NASCAR's youngest rookie, Jamie 'Jinx Junior' Hammond, and teammate Cole Whaling.

"The pair were reportedly mixed up in an early-morning wrestling match with two women in the parking lot of Daytona's infamous Bar None. 'You should have seen Jamie blush when I kissed him,' said Penny Plithton. 'It was so cute.'

"Though it is believed that alcohol was not a factor, the antics have caused problems with the 56 team's sponsor, Food Basket. Owner Leo Farmer is quoted as saying, 'We expect the driver we sponsor to demonstrate the best in family values, just as our company does. This incident has us very concerned. We intend to look into it very carefully in order to determine whether Mr. Hammond is the right match for Food Basket.'

"Reaction continues to ripple throughout the NASCAR community. Stay tuned for more information after HRI's press conference, scheduled for 10:00 a.m. tomorrow."

"WHAT THE HELL were you thinking?" Kellie paced in front of Cole and Jamie, slapping a rolled up newspaper against her palm. "Have you totally lost your collective minds?"

"Mom, I can explain," Jamie began.

Cole offered his most appealing smile. "It's all my fault, Kellie."

"I don't doubt that for a minute."

His smile faltered, then faded altogether, and he released a sigh. "Okay, you're right. I shouldn't have taken him out. I was just trying to cheer him up. It was his first race and he crashed. You must have seen the news clips when the press jumped him on his way out of the hospital. He needed to get away from the craziness and put things in perspective."

Fury skyrocketed through her. "By playing pool with a pair of barflies? Have you lost your mind?" she repeated, though at a slightly higher decibel level. If there weren't the full width of the conference table separating them, she would have strangled him. "You took an eighteen-year-old boy to a bar. A bar, Cole!"

"I didn't drink," Jamie hastened to say.

"And it's a good thing you didn't," Kellie snapped. "Or it would have brought a short career to a fast end. NASCAR takes a very dim view of underage drinking." Her gaze switched to Cole. "As I'm sure you're well aware."

He winced. "No one was supposed to find out."

"Which brings us back to those women. If no one

was supposed to find out, then maybe you shouldn't have bragged about who you were."

"It might have been a mistake to tell Penny the truth," Cole conceded.

"Why not, when your fame guaranteed you their full attention?" Her sarcasm left him wincing.

"I'm sorry, Kellie," he repeated.

There was no mistaking his sincerity. She'd known Cole a long time and had learned over the years to distinguish between his trying-to-get-out-of-it song-and-dance and those few times when he allowed his playboy facade to drop and reveal the "real" Cole. He'd always had a soft spot for Jamie, and she couldn't see him deliberately harming the boy.

"It wouldn't have been so bad if that had been the end of it." She thrust a hand through her hair. "Though I can't even believe I'm even admitting that much. But then you had to compound the problem by—" She checked the paper. "Piggyback wrestling in the parking lot. Whatever that is."

"See, the girls get on our shoulders and they wrestle while we try and hold them," Jamie offered helpfully.

"Enough!" It took every ounce of self-control to keep from utterly losing it. "That's not the point, Jamie. You have a morals clause in your contract, and though this didn't breach it, you're bumping up against it. Leo Farmer has already called three times so far this morning. I could hear Stephanie crying in the background."

Jamie went dead white. "Stephanie heard about last night?"

"Haven't you been listening to a word I've been saying?" There were times when her son seemed so mature. And then the next instant, he'd revert to being a typical teenager. She closed her eyes. Well, how could she blame him? He was a teenager. She reined in her temper and spoke as gently as possible. "Honey, you've been around this business all your life, certainly long enough to know that the entire world hears about something this…harebrained. You're under a microscope now. We explained that to you when we first starting talking about moving you to NASCAR."

She might as well have saved her breath. He'd switched off the instant she'd mentioned Stephanie's name. "I need to talk to her," he insisted. He would have raced from the room if Kellie hadn't stopped him.

"First you need to talk to Leo Farmer and offer an apology so he doesn't pull his sponsorship. And then you're going to work with our PR people drafting a statement that properly reflects the depth of your remorse. Once that's done, and if Leo gives his permission, and *if* Stephanie even wants to speak to you, you may get in touch with her. Are we clear?"

"But Stephanie—"

She hardened herself against his pleading, inserting a steely note in her voice. "Assuming Leo lets you anywhere near his daughter again, which is highly doubtful, you can grovel to your heart's content. In the meantime, I've explained what you're to do."

Jamie nodded. "Yes, Mrs. Hammond. I'll take care of it right away."

If Kellie hadn't understood that he was using the title as a way to acknowledge that their current role was employer/employee versus mother/son, she'd have found a way to ground him until he turned twenty-one. "Mistakes happen," she acknowledged. "Drivers who last in this business learn from them and work very hard not to make the same one twice."

He gave her a stiff nod. "Is that it?"

A bone-deep weariness gripped her. "You can go now."

"Me, too?" Cole asked as Jamie made a beeline for the door. "Or do you want to shout at me for a while longer?"

"I'd like to take a stick to that thick head of yours," she snapped.

He nodded. "I don't blame you." He circled the table and edged a hip on the heavy oak surface in front of where she stood. "This won't happen again, Kellie, I promise. I was trying to take him under my wing." He spared her a teasing smile. "Unfortunately, I forgot that I don't have wings. Just horns."

Her mouth twitched. "I know you meant well. But even so—"

To her surprise, he reached out and swept a lock of hair behind her ear. "I don't mean to add to your stress. I know how rough it's been without Jinx. I'd like to help, not make matters worse."

"Thanks, Cole. I appreciate that." She started to take a step backward. Before she could, he caught her hand in his, anchoring her in place.

"I just want you to know I'm here for you. If you need anything, anything at all, you only have to ask."

She tugged her hand free, softening the rejection with a smile. "Again, I appreciate that. We've worked together for a long time. You're like family."

"Kissing cousins?" he offered lightly.

She regarded him warily. "What's going on, Cole?"

He tipped his head to one side and flashed his dimples at her. "You want me to be frank?"

"Please."

"I've always been attracted to you, Kellie," he shocked her by saying. "It's been growing for years now."

Oh, no. No, no, no. "I never—"

He held up his hand, cutting her off. "You never once looked sideways at me. It was always Jinx and I respect that. I just need you to know how I feel."

She bit her lip. How had they gone from a reprimand to this? He'd caught her totally off guard. "Cole, I'm at a loss for words. It's only been a couple of months since Jinx died."

Something altered his easygoing expression, a hardness that startled her, almost a bitterness. He took her hand in his again. "You're still a young woman. A woman who hasn't had the sort of marital relationship she might have wished for."

She snatched her hand from his hold. "That's enough. My marriage to Jinx is none of your business."

"Fine. I didn't mean to offend you." He grew more serious than she'd ever seen him. "But I want more, Kellie."

"What do you mean?"

"I mean I'm coming up on contract negotiations and I want more than to be your driver. I want you, as well." He eyed her with open speculation. "I'll give you anything you ask, sweetheart. Anything and everything your heart desires. A ring. Marriage. More children, if you want."

She stared in utter shock. He couldn't be serious. She started shaking her head before he'd even finished speaking. "It's too much, too soon. I'm not ready for any of this. I can't deal with it right now."

To her relief, he didn't argue. "Okay. I can understand that. So here's what I'm proposing." His hazel eyes darkened, the gold highlights taking on a tarnished sheen. "Think about my offer. Over the next few months, let's get together on occasion and see how it goes. Maybe it'll help you to stop thinking about me as your driver, and start looking at me as a man."

She didn't dare tell him that she already saw him as a man. He was simply a man who didn't appeal. He never had and never would. There'd only been one man who, with a single, smoldering look, had her thinking of darkened bedrooms and passionate lovemaking. Only one man who'd tempted her into foolishness as a teenager, and who could still tempt her to repeat that foolishness now.

"Okay, Cole. I'll think about what you've said." Anything to put an end to their conversation. "But I can't make any promises."

"I'm not asking for any. Yet…" he added pointedly. "In the meantime, why don't you let me take care of one of your problems. It'll be my gift to you, no strings attached."

Something about the way he said that had her internal alarms going off. "What problem?"

"Lucas."

Just that one word, but she instantly knew what he meant. She shook her head. "No, Cole. Absolutely not."

He leaned in and lowered his voice. "He only gets controlling interest of HRI if he wins the NASCAR Championship. I can ensure he doesn't."

"I said no and I meant no." She swept away from him. "Lucas is an integral part of this organization and I don't want to hear another word about this. Ever."

He held up his hands and offered a dazzling smile. "I hear you."

Oh, God. She knew that look, had heard that tone used countless times before. It meant he understood, but intended to do what he wanted, regardless. "No, I don't think you do," she retorted with a hint of desperation. "I'm dead serious here. You keep your hands—and more importantly, your bumper—off Lucas Boyce. Are we clear?"

He assumed a somber expression that struck her as patently fake. "You got it, boss. I understand perfectly. Hear no evil, see no evil."

It was all Kellie could do to keep from ripping out her hair. "Cole—"

He laughed. "I'm just messing with you." He put his hand over his heart. "I promise on my honor that I won't put a bumper to Bad. Satisfied?"

Somewhat mollified, she nodded. "Thanks."

He straightened. Approached. "But I can't promise

not to put a bumper to you, Kellie. Fair warning. I'm coming after you."

"I—" She was saved from a reply by a brisk rap on the door.

Lucas stuck his head in. "Got a minute?"

Intense relief flooded through her. "Sure. We're done here."

Cole stiffened, a spark of something that might have been anger leaping into his eyes. "Are we done?" he murmured.

"Was there something else?" she asked with formal briskness, hoping he'd get the message.

He released his breath in a sigh. "I guess not. Just remember what I said."

"I will, if you will."

Lucas waited until Cole had left the room before looking at Kellie. He lifted an eyebrow. "What's going on?"

She managed a smile, though the memory of the kiss they'd shared two nights before made it difficult to think clearly. Her gaze slid to his mouth and she couldn't seem to shift her attention, no matter how hard she tried. He'd tasted so amazing, overwhelming her senses from that first incredible touch. And it hadn't been just his mouth. It had been how his body had felt against hers, the power and strength of his arms around her, the delicious sweep of his hands molding her close. If they'd been anywhere other than in a hospital, she'd have been totally and utterly swept away.

He must have sensed the direction of her thoughts.

His smile grew, his expression too shrewd for her liking. "Problem?" he asked, his voice low and intimate.

She'd lost her mind. There wasn't any other explanation for her lapse. Using every ounce of remaining willpower, she forced herself to switch gears, starting with tearing her gaze from his mouth. Spinning on her heel, she swept to the far side of her office. "I'm just having trouble adjusting to my new role. In the past, Jinx handled the discipline while I took care of the business end of things."

"Discipline?"

"I had a talk with Cole and Jamie about their activities last night." She faced him with a grimace. "It wasn't pleasant."

"You spoke to them without me?"

The question chased away any lingering remnants of desire, and she stilled. "Yes, I talked to them without you." Her eyebrows drew together in the suggestion of a frown. "You don't really think you should have been there, do you?"

He matched her frown with one of his own. "I'm a partner in the firm. What causes trouble for HRI causes trouble for me." Turning, he closed the door, closeting them in her office. "If nothing else, we should have discussed how to handle the situation beforehand. Even if you didn't want me to address either of them directly, I should have sat in on the conversation so it was clear our response was a joint one."

"I don't agree. Neither of them would have responded well to having you witness that particular conversation."

"That's a distinct possibility. Nonetheless, we should have had a conversation before you made a unilateral decision."

As much as she'd like to argue that fact, she couldn't. "Fair enough," she conceded. "Next time I will."

To her relief, he let it go, turning the conversation in a slightly different direction. "This aspect of the business isn't going to get any easier, Kellie, even with my input on the various decisions you make. If I win the NASCAR Championship this year and take controlling interest, you'll still need to deal with some of the personality issues when they crop up, mainly because I'm a fellow driver and someone they clearly regard as an interloper. They'll take any disciplinary actions a hell of a lot better from you than from me."

"Jamie might listen to you."

Lucas shook his head. "Not even Jamie. I'm not his father and he wouldn't appreciate my acting as if I am."

"You're right, of course. From now on I'll consider discipline part of my duties, and I'll discuss issues like this with you before I take action." To her relief her voice remained cool and calm, but she didn't trust it to stay that way much longer. She deliberately changed the subject. "So, what did you need me for?" she asked. "Another problem?"

"Forget it. This isn't the right time. Not after the morning you've had."

"You have no idea," she said with a bit too much feeling, and instantly realized she'd made a mistake.

"Was there something more going on than last

night's fun and games?" Lucas's eyes narrowed in clear assessment. "You were talking to Cole when I walked in. Not Jamie and Cole. Just Cole. Was that still about last night, or do we have another partnership issue the two of us need to discuss?"

She didn't dare tell him the particulars of her conversation with Cole, or mention either of the suggestions he'd made. His personal proposition had been shocking enough. But if she dared repeat the one regarding Lucas, it would guarantee a full-blown brawl, something she'd do anything to avoid.

She dismissed Lucas's question with a casual wave of her hand. "It's nothing I can't handle."

If anything her comment had Lucas's expression hardening. "What's going on, Kellie?"

"Just contract negotiations." She took a seat behind her desk and pulled a file toward her. "Cole's up for renewal at the end of this season."

Lucas didn't say anything for a long moment. "In case it's escaped your notice, that would fall under the heading of partnership discussion. Serious partnership discussion, to be exact."

"I wouldn't agree to any contractual issues without your agreement."

"Correction, Mrs. Hammond." He planted his hands on her desk and leaned in. "You won't so much as discuss contractual issues without my presence, as well as my agreement."

Kellie released a soft sigh. "Do we have to do this now?"

"Yeah, I think we do." He straightened and she could tell he was deciding how best to deal with her. "You and I have an interesting, if turbulent history. Maybe we should get some of our personal issues out into the open and resolve whatever's still lingering between us."

His comment gave her the opening she needed to deal with what had happened two nights ago, to put it behind them once and for all. She darted a swift glance in his direction, attempting to assess his mood. As usual, he was next to impossible to read. Years ago she'd had far better success. But that had been before his meteoric rise in the racing world…and his marriage to Bridgette.

Kellie still remembered the pain of hearing the announcement on the news. There'd been a shot of the happy couple, the gorgeous blue-eyed blonde beaming into the camera while Lucas had maintained an impassively remote visage, most of his expression hidden behind his signature shades.

"She looks a bit like you," Jinx had offered gruffly. "Not as refined. But there's a passing resemblance."

She'd forced an amused look and asked, "Don't men have weaknesses for a certain type?"

"Sometimes," he conceded. "Cole, for instance. But I've never noticed that about Lucas." He hesitated, adding in a low voice, "Have you ever regretted it, Kellie?"

She crossed to his side. Dropping beside his wheelchair, she gathered his hands in hers. "Do I regret the affair I had with him? No. It was a special night. One I'll never forget. And it gave me a son, a son who's one of the true delights in my life."

"And me? Do you regret marrying me?"

She shook her head, offering Jinx a loving smile. "Not even a little. You're the best thing that ever happened to me. Without you—" Tears filled her eyes. "I don't know what I'd have done."

He still appeared troubled. "You could have approached Lucas and told him you were pregnant with his child."

It was a suggestion she'd heard before, and one she'd always been quick to quash in no uncertain terms. "Not a chance. He made his feelings crystal clear the morning after. From day one he was focused on his career and only his career."

"Not only."

She flushed. "Fine. With the occasional distractions. But his career has always come first. That hasn't changed, despite what Bridgette might think." She spared a swift, pained peek at the television screen. "She'll find out soon enough."

"If he'd known about Jamie…" He gathered her face in his hands. She'd never seen him so somber. "It's not the same when you're talking about a child. It makes a difference, honey."

Would it have? Probably, but not the way Jinx meant. She knew Lucas. His sense of duty was a mile wide. He'd have quit racing in order to make sure his wife and child were provided for. She couldn't allow him to do that. Not then. And now… Well, now it was too late. Too much time had gone by. They'd both moved on with their lives.

"You've commented on his dedication, yourself,

Jinx," she'd said. "You and Dad have both said you've never seen a driver more committed to his career. He wouldn't have won his sixth NASCAR Championship and be heading toward a record-tying seventh if he hadn't been. When he first started out, a wife and child would have gotten in his way. He didn't have the maturity or the vision to see past it the way you did."

"But it would have been his choice. You should have told him."

She bowed her head. "You don't understand. I couldn't."

"Why not?"

She hesitated, not certain how much she should reveal. Finally, she admitted, "He told me something that next morning, something that explained why his career was so important to him. I couldn't do anything to ruin that for him." She took a deep breath, gathering her self-control. "It would have destroyed the man he was if I'd taken that away from him."

"He could have still raced."

"He would have felt obligated to get a 'real' job, one with a steady paycheck and benefits." Her shoulders jerked in a helpless shrug. "I couldn't do that to him."

Jinx's attention switched to the television screen. "Things have changed since then. Looks like he's feeling secure enough now. Secure enough to have a wife and still race." He lifted an eyebrow. "What if he gives Jamie a brother or sister? What then?"

The image roused emotions that should have been long dead, emotions that threatened to crush her. It took every ounce of self-possession to hold them at bay. "We'll let him have his happiness, just as we have ours." She covered her husband's hands with her own. "We have each other, Jinx. Best of all, we have Jamie. We made a family. We built HRI from scratch. And since Cole joined the team, we have one of the best drivers on the circuit. I'm not dissatisfied. Are you?"

He gently turned her face toward him and feathered a kiss across her mouth. "Not at all." His expression grew grave. "But are you happy?"

She offered him a tremulous smile. "I couldn't be happier."

The memory faded and Kellie stared at Lucas, remembering the kiss she'd shared with him, comparing it to the kisses she and Jinx had exchanged over the years. She realized now that she'd been lying to her husband, even if she hadn't been aware of it at the time.

She'd been happy, after a fashion. But it hadn't been the sort of ecstatic happiness she'd sensed she would have known with Lucas. Jinx had taught her about friendship, and the deep and abiding love that came from that. But it hadn't been a soul-deep everlasting passion. At least, not the sort of love that a wife should have felt for her husband.

Now, after all these years, Lucas was in her life again. And he wanted to resolve their differences, no doubt to make his position within the HRI organization more comfortable. Well, she couldn't blame him for that.

She chose her words with care. "I appreciate your

wanting to involve yourself in all aspects of HRI. As a partner in the firm, you should. But when it comes to the two of us, I think we need to keep our relationship strictly business. The other night was an aberration. It can't happen again."

"Is that what you consider our kiss?" he asked blandly. "An aberration?"

She gave him a direct look in return. "That's all I want it to be. It can't be anything else. You're my driver, as well as my partner. There's a possibility that you'll have controlling interest of HRI before the end of the year. Things are complicated enough without making it any worse."

"Worse?"

She waved that aside. "You know what I mean. I don't have time for a personal relationship. Not with you."

"And not with Cole?"

Had he seen something? she wondered in alarm. Sensed it? "And not with Cole," she concurred evenly. "Not that it would be any of your business if I did."

"Point taken." He came around her desk. Before she could do more than utter a small gasp of alarm, he scooped her out of her chair and into his arms. "But allow me to make one more point. You might think we can keep our relationship pure business. But there's a small, vital detail you've overlooked."

She eyed him warily. "What detail?"

"This one."

She didn't have the chance to offer more than a token objection. He molded his mouth to hers, a hungry groan rumbling deep in his chest. She responded to that sound on an instinctive level. Unable to help herself, she opened to him and melted slowly into his embrace. She found herself standing on her own two feet again, although given how weak her legs were, she wasn't sure how it was physically possible. The kiss deepened beneath his insistent invasion. It was a brand of possession, man reverting to his most primal essence. Uncontrollable desire swept through her, filling her with the urge to take all he had to give.

Her hands stole across the breadth of his shoulders and the well-defined contours of his chest. She'd steal these few treasured seconds and explore the territory she'd once known so well. Discover each and every change the years had wrought. Dear heaven, how had she managed to live so long without this? And now that he'd reminded her of all she'd forced herself to forget, how could she walk away again?

It was that awareness, the memory of the crippling pain she'd experienced the last time they'd parted, that brought her to her senses. She ripped free of his embrace. "Stop it, Lucas. We can't do this. Not again. It was a mistake the first time and it's a worse mistake now."

"I don't agree."

A fierce determination took hold and he leaned into her, telling her without words of his intent. He gave her enough time to pull away, to escape the inevitable. But she couldn't, not when his mouth gentled her with a kiss so tender and so thorough that it melted every ounce of resistance.

This time there was a newness to his taking, as though he were starting over. As though all that had gone before had been wiped clean. She was seventeen again and kissing him for the first time. And yet there was a familiarity there, a delicious sensuality that spoke of maturity and experience and a knowledge of how to fulfill a woman's deepest, most closely held needs.

In his arms, in that moment, Kellie came completely undone, surrendering to him just as she had all those years ago. The minute he sensed that surrender, he broke the kiss, leaving her in a world of unfulfilled want.

"Tell me that was a mistake," he murmured against her mouth. And with that, he left the room.

CHAPTER SEVEN

"WELL, FANS, we've made it through the first four weeks of racing and it's been full of nonstop action and hijinks. We've had crunches and crashes, fines and penalties, bumper-to-bumper finishes and a guaranteed win stolen by a final lap crash.

"We've also seen our youngest NASCAR NEXTEL Cup driver dealing with the family curse. Yes, folks, despite some impressive finishes that have moved Jinx Junior into the top half of the points standing, the youngster continues to be plagued by the run of bad luck that followed his famous father throughout Jinx's stellar career. Bad pit stops, blown tires and, of course, that spectacular crash at Daytona, have left fans hoping for the best for NASCAR's latest teen heartthrob…but fearing the worst!"

"HEY, KID, WAIT UP."

The sound of Cole's voice had Jamie pausing outside his Bristol garage. Ever since that night after the Daytona race, he'd done his best to maintain a friendly, if safe, distance from his fellow driver. He suspected Cole knew it, too. But if it bothered the older driver, he hadn't let on.

"Problem?" Jamie asked.

Cole dropped a companionable arm around Jamie's shoulders and ushered him away from the noise and activity surrounding the garages. "Listen. I've been meaning to apologize to you for a while now."

"Forget it. It's over."

At least, Jamie hoped so. It had taken a lot of work to recover some of the ground he'd lost. After four weeks of being on his best behavior, he still hadn't fully regained Leo Farmer's trust. And even Stephanie would glance at him periodically with a worried frown that made him want to kick himself for having been so stupid.

Cole grimaced. "Yeah, well. I wasn't thinking about the consequences of our little adventure and I should have. I thought we'd let off some steam and instead I got you into serious trouble. I'm really sorry." He lifted an eyebrow. "We good? You're not too ticked off with me?"

Jamie relaxed, slipping back into the old, familiar relationship the two of them had shared before the season had started. "Sure. We're cool."

"What about your sponsor? Food Basket giving you grief?"

"Leo Farmer watches me like a hawk." Jamie shrugged. "But that's only to be expected."

"Rough deal." Cole scraped a hand along his jaw. "I've been in a predicament or two over the years. Mind if I make a suggestion?"

"So long as it doesn't involve piggyback wrestling, I'd appreciate it."

Cole grinned. "I think we both learned our lesson

with that one." His smile faded. "It's real simple. Grovel, apologize, talk it through. Do whatever it takes, so long as you're up-front with them from now on. You can't fake your way out of this one, kid. You have to mean it or Farmer will see right through you."

"But, I do mean it."

Cole nodded in satisfaction. "Then you're halfway there. Just keep it up and they'll ease off in time."

Jamie felt reluctant to risk the next question, but there wasn't anyone else he felt comfortable asking. "There's just one thing I'm not sure how to handle."

"I don't suppose her name is Stephanie?"

Jamie ducked his head and grinned. "It might be."

"She's Farmer's daughter, isn't she?"

"Yeah. She's wonderful. Sweet. Smart. Pretty."

"Let me be frank with you, kid. Having an affair with a sponsor's daughter is risky."

Jamie could feel himself turning brick-red. "We're not having an affair," he muttered.

"Might as well be." Cole paused by the pit wall and took a seat. "You need to understand something. You decide to date the Stephanies in this world, you're going to wake up one day with a leash attached to the collar you're suddenly wearing. Once she's got that collar on you, one wrong move and you're tagged, bagged and smiling up at the coroner. The way I see it, you've got two choices."

Jamie perched on the wall next to the other driver. "Stop piggyback wrestling?"

Cole laughed. "That would be one."

"And the other?"

"Ditch her. She's not worth the aggravation."

Jamie stared in shock. "No way. I really like her."

"Then we're back to option one. You need to be on your best behavior." Cole winked. "Got it?"

Relaxing ever so slightly, Jamie nodded. "Got it. Thanks."

"Since I'm responsible for your being in this mess, giving you a few pointers is the least I can do." He hesitated. "I've got to tell you, one of the things that's been bothering me most about all this is the trouble we've caused your mom." A frown creased his brow. "Although I have an idea how you can make it up to her."

Jamie went on instant alert. He'd felt nothing but guilt over just that issue. If Cole had a solution, he was all over it. "What? What can I do?"

"Nah, forget it. She wouldn't appreciate my mentioning it."

"I won't tell her."

Cole shot Jamie a look that had him stiffening in alarm. "I'm serious, kid. This has to stay strictly between the two of us."

"Absolutely."

Cole made a point of glancing around. "Have you noticed that we're sitting at one of the best short tracks on the circuit? And Martinsville will be next week. Another top-notch short track."

Jamie nodded. Despite his confusion at the change in subject, he couldn't conceal his enthusiasm. "I can't wait. I've always done well at short track racing."

"I seem to remember a few races where you were able to put the bumper to your competition and move them out of the way without incurring the wrath of any of the officials. It was smooth. Very smooth."

"Right..." Jamie shook his head in bewilderment. "So?"

"So, you know how easy it is to get into someone, accidentally, of course," he hastened to add. "Seems like a good opportunity to move one of your current competitors out of the way with no one being the wiser." At Jamie's continued look of bafflement, a hint of exasperation crept into Cole's voice. "You like the idea of someone coming in and stealing your inheritance, kid? Or do you want to make sure that doesn't happen?"

Jamie couldn't conceal his shock. "You mean... wreck Bad? On purpose?"

"Did I say that? I said *accidentally*. I distinctly heard myself say it. Just accidentally enough to maybe knock him out of the top twelve in points." Cole clapped Jamie on the shoulder. "Think about it. I guarantee your mother would appreciate it. Unless you want her to lose the business?"

With that pointed jab, the older driver stood and walked off, leaving Jamie more confused than he'd been before Cole had approached. One question remained uppermost in his mind.

What did he do now?

"RELAX, KELLIE. I'm not going to attack you."

Lucas stepped into her motor home and watched in

amusement as warm color saturated her cheeks. For the past four weeks—ever since Daytona—she'd been a bundle of nerves whenever they'd been alone together. Maybe it was that kiss, that amazing, incredible kiss they'd shared in her office. He'd expected the hit he'd taken physically from their embrace. But he hadn't expected the other consequences that had come with it.

First there'd been the overwhelming need to have her again. To kiss her. To hold her. To touch every inch of her.

But of more concern than the physical were the sensations he had whenever they were together. As often as he attempted to deny it, there was an emotional element surging just beneath the surface. Dangerous emotions. Emotions he had no right to feel. Emotions he had no intention of experiencing ever again. He'd been burned twice by women he'd misread. He wouldn't allow it to happen ever again. Particularly with this woman.

"I didn't think you were going to attack me," she instantly denied. "I just didn't expect you."

"I wouldn't be here, except we've got a problem," Lucas informed her.

"Of course we do."

She released a sigh, rubbing the nape of her neck. She often wore her hair up when she worked. Maybe she thought it gave her a more businesslike appearance. As far as he was concerned, piling all that weight on top of her head made her look more fragile, the hairstyle emphasized the vulnerable sweep of her neck.

"Have a seat." She gestured toward the couch. "Tell me what's wrong."

He made himself comfortable on the thick leather cushions. Leaning forward, he rested his forearms on his knees and held her with a direct look. "You have to bite the bullet and fire Jamie's crew chief. It's not working out and you need someone who knows what they're doing here and at Martinsville."

He'd caught her off guard and she shook her head in denial. "Lucky's been in this business for—"

He cut to the chase. "Lucky has a drinking problem."

"You can't be serious," she replied in clear disbelief.

"I'm dead serious."

"How do you know? Did you see him drinking on the job?"

"Not on the job, no."

"Afterward?"

"Yes."

She dismissed that with a hint of exasperation. "He's not the only employee to lift a bottle when he's off duty. If I fired people for that, we'd lose most of the men in the garage."

"Lucky's found an unfortunate way to deal with the stress of his job. He's under too much pressure."

She waved that aside. "We all are."

He tried again. "This jinx nonsense the media is perpetuating…it affects the team as much as Jamie. You must realize that the Hammond Jinx doesn't just impact the driver. All the men feel jinxed. And that makes them clumsy. Lucky's solution is to escape into a bottle. And

I don't mean a beer or two after work. I'm talking about some serious bootleg stuff. The kind that'll rot your gut and make you blind."

Kellie fought back a smile. "His father was a moonshiner. Lucky says that any liquor with a label is nothing more than baby's milk in comparison."

He lifted an eyebrow. "And that doesn't set off alarm bells?"

"I'll speak to him. Will that do?"

Lucas shook his head. "Not even a little." He dropped his head as he considered how best to reason with her without getting her back up. "I know this is tough, Kellie. I know you don't want to have to fire someone who's been part of HRI for so many years."

"He's been with the company from the start. Before HRI, he was Jinx's jackman. You're asking me to make this decision without having anything to go on other than your suspicions."

"How long have I been in this business, Kellie?"

"Okay, I get the point. That doesn't change the facts. Bring me someone who smelled alcohol on him during a race or during business hours. Until you do, I'm not willing to upset things without cause. He and Jamie are close. They're comfortable with each other."

Lucas tried a different approach. "Are you aware that Lucky does nothing to dispel the Jinx Junior label? If anything, he encourages it. Why do you suppose that is?"

A hint of anger sparked in her eyes. "I have no idea. But I suspect you're going to tell me it's because he's drinking."

"It's to help cover his drinking. If the team is jinxed, little mistakes that might have been caught get over-looked because it's not the crew chief. It's not his drinking. It's the jinx. Everyone's so focused on that, they ignore what's right in front of their faces."

He could see her considering, running through some of the problems they'd had with Jamie's setup over the past few weeks. "He's done well," she murmured, as though trying to convince herself. "The problems have actually been minor. The media—"

"Has taken great delight in blowing them into major issues. I won't argue with that. But ask yourself this…" He waited until he had her full attention. "Do you believe in the jinx?"

"Of course not," she instantly replied.

"No jinx? You're positive? No possibility of Jamie having inherited his father's bad luck?"

For some reason the question had a shadow drifting across her expression. "He didn't inherit Jinx's ques-tionable luck," she stated in no uncertain terms. "There's not a doubt in my mind."

"Then why's the team having so many problems?"

"They've never worked together before, Lucas. It takes time to shake out all the kinks."

"Granted, but—"

"I'm not making a change this close to the race," she informed him flatly. She rose and headed to the refrig-erator. Jerking it open, she grabbed two bottles of water. Tossing him the first, she cracked the second and took a long swallow. She glared at him as she recapped the bottle. "Damn it, Lucas. I've been in the war wagon with Lucky every single race since the start of the season. Don't you think I'd have caught on if he'd been drinking?"

"You have a lot on your plate right now. It's easy to overlook things when so many other issues have priority. It's even easier to miss them when they're deliberately being kept from you." He frowned. "You've had to take on a lot since Jinx died."

She took instant offense. "I worked alongside Jinx for a lot of years, Lucas. I can handle it."

"But you told me there were certain areas of the business that he controlled exclusively. Discipline, for instance."

He could see her reluctance to answer. Finally she jerked her head in an abrupt nod. "Discipline. The teams and shop. I handled sponsors, PR, and supervised the accounting end of things."

He should have stepped in sooner to help out, would have if he hadn't been so intent on treading lightly and making his transition into the company as smooth as possible. But it would seem the time had come to yank off the velvet gloves. "You need to allow me to fill the hole that Jinx's death has left."

She started shaking her head before he'd even finished. "I'm in charge. It's my responsibility to keep HRI running."

"Listen to me, *partner.* One person cannot run a business of this magnitude."

"One person doesn't," she corrected. She started

ticking off on her fingers. "I have a business manager, a general manager, an operation manager, accountants, lawyers, engineers, any number of assistants, a PR and marketing department—"

"All of whom report to you. How many meetings a week do you take? Hell, how many a day?" He thrust a hand through his hair. "I've seen your office light on into the wee hours of the morning. You can't cover every aspect, Kellie. You need to shift some of the load."

"To you." It wasn't a question.

"Yes. I'm your partner, remember?"

Her mouth twitched in a wry smile. "I keep forgetting that."

Standing, he tugged some folded papers from his pocket. "Here."

If the circumstances had been different, he'd have laughed at her undisguised wariness. "What's that?" she asked.

Since she didn't make a move to take the papers, he crossed to where she stood. Taking her hand in his, he slapped typed pages into her palm. "This is the part of the business I'll be taking responsibility for starting the Monday we get back from Bristol."

She took immediate offense and her hand balled around the pages, crumpling them. "You have no right—"

"I have every right and you know it. Look over the list. Most of it has to do with the mechanical end of things, just like Jinx. I've divided things up so we're each handling the areas that play to our individual strengths. If there's anything on there you want to wrangle over, I'm willing to listen."

"Just not agree."

Unable to resist, he caught her close. "Glad we understand each other."

"Don't," she protested. "Someone might come in."

"If that's your only concern…" He maneuvered her so he could reach the door to the motor home and throw the lock. "That should give us a few minutes of privacy."

"That's not the point." She closed her eyes, hiding the want that had been lurking there. "We're business partners, with the emphasis on business. If that's not enough incentive for you, maybe you should remember that we made this mistake years ago and should have enough age and experience on us to know better than to let it happen again. And if *that's* not enough, there's one more consideration."

"Jinx."

She looked at him, the wealth of pain and sorrow impacting like a physical blow. "Yes."

"You want me."

"Yes," she said again. A heartbreaking smile edged her mouth. "But I've learned over the years that there are lots of things I want that I can't have. You're just one more. You always have been."

He should step away and let her go. It was the sensible thing to do. But he'd never been sensible. He'd spent the past two decades earning the nickname "Bad" the hard way and he didn't see that changing, not while he had a woman like Kellie in his arms.

The only difference this time around was that they both knew what they were getting into. No more blindsiding. What happened after this would be nothing more than an affair. They were at a stage in their lives where they could enjoy each other physically, without needing the emotional entanglement that tripped the unwary.

He cupped her face and saw the apprehension she couldn't quite conceal. "It's okay, Kellie," he murmured. "We won't screw it up this time."

He took her mouth, slow and thorough. God, she tasted amazing—sweet and eager and almost as aggressive as he was. Her arms slid around his neck, her fingers forking into his hair. She tilted her head to one side and deepened the kiss, changing it on an elemental level. It took a minute to comprehend the difference. And then it hit him.

She was by nature more generous than he, and that quality showed in her kiss. Where he took, she gave. Where he demanded, she coaxed. Where he conquered, she seduced. Soft overcoming hard. Gentleness defusing the aggression. The tenderness of a woman overcoming the roughness of man.

It drove him wild.

He pulled back, his voice dipping low and rough and hungry. "Oh, yeah. We'll definitely get it right this time. We're not kids anymore. We both know the score."

He felt a ripple of tension skitter through her and a hint of a frown pinched her eyebrows together. "Just so I'm clear…what score is that, Lucas?"

"We're adults. Neither of us is married. Who's to

care if we indulge in an affair? We'll get whatever's going on between us out of our systems once and for all."

"Get it out of our systems," she repeated. "Like it's a…I don't know…a virus that needs to run its course? Is that how you're looking at this?"

He regarded her warily. "Not a virus, no. Call it chemistry, if you rather. Whatever it is, it's strong and it's physical and there's absolutely no reason why we can't indulge."

"Until it runs its course."

He hardened himself to the hint of pain that underscored her comment. "That's what happens with affairs. You know that. They start out hot and heavy, but time cools the flames. If we go into this with our eyes open, it won't interfere with the business end of things."

"While our affair lasts."

"You're ticked off."

"Aren't you the observant one," she marveled.

He laughed, the sound short and harsh. "Hell, and here I didn't think I could be blindsided by you again." He planted his hands on her shoulders and leaned in so she wouldn't miss a single word. "You haven't changed at all, have you, Kellie? You're still into fantasy. And here I am right back in the middle of it. Well, pay attention, sweetheart. You want to scratch your itch, I'm the man. But if you're still looking for that white picket fence and happily-ever-after ending, look somewhere else."

"Thank you," she said with a haughty formality that

had him seeing red. "I'll do just that. In the meantime, I want you to take your hands off me. And I don't want you to touch me ever again. I don't care if I'm about to fall off the war wagon into oncoming traffic, keep your hands off me. Clear?"

"Oh, yeah. Perfectly."

"Excellent." Ripping free of his embrace, she bent and picked up the papers he'd handed her earlier. She made a production of smoothing them out. "I'll be certain to give these the attention they deserve. And I'll also consider what you had to say about Lucky." She took two entire seconds to scan his list before balling the papers into a wad and lobbing them toward the nearest trash can. "There. I've considered and filed them where they'll do the most good. And just so we're clear, Lucky stays on as Jamie's crew chief."

"Careful, Mrs. Hammond," he warned. "I only allow someone to push so far. And then I start pushing back."

He didn't bother to wait for her response, which was probably a good thing since he suspected the word she uttered as he slammed the door wasn't a compliment. He also suspected it was one he richly deserved.

CHAPTER EIGHT

"WITH FANS LOOKING forward to the roar of Bristol, one question on everyone's minds is, 'Who broke the Hammond family mirrors?' Jamie 'Jinx Junior' Hammond has broken hearts and boundaries, but so far he has yet to break the infamous Hammond Curse, started by his father, late racing legend Jinx Hammond. If this young driver wants to step out from the shadow of experienced teammates Cole Whaling and Lucas 'Bad' Boyce, he'll have to clean up his act, pull out in front of the pack, and be the first to stop that black cat from crossing the track."

"DON'T LET THEM get to you, Jamie." Stephanie caught his hand in hers as they strolled through Bristol's garage area. "You're not a jinx."

"It's not that."

How could he tell her what was really going through his mind? How could he tell her how he'd agonized all day over Cole's suggestion that he put Lucas in the wall at some point during the race?

She fixed him with an unblinking stare, her dark eyes seeming to see straight through him. "Then what's wrong?"

He shrugged uneasily. "Just something Cole and I were talking about earlier," he said.

A hint of worry crept into her expression. "Do you want to go out clubbing with him again?"

Jamie paused midstride and tugged her to a stop. He cupped her sweet face in his hands and stared down with utter sincerity. "I'm not even a little interested. I promised you I'd never do that again and I won't."

"It's your choice," she hastened to assure him. "I won't try and stop you."

"I know you wouldn't. But that's not the point, is it?" He'd worked so hard to earn her trust again. Did she really think he'd do anything to jeopardize that? "I know that if I were that stupid again, you'd break up with me. And I wouldn't blame you, either."

Relieved, she offered a quick, teasing smile. "Well, you're right about one thing. You can't piggyback wrestle with other women and have me, too."

"Other women don't interest me. You're the only one I want."

She returned to her original question with infuriating tenacity. "So, if this isn't about going out with Cole, then what's bothering you?"

Jamie shook his head in amused exasperation. "If my focus were as good as yours, I'd have won a race already."

She lifted up onto tiptoe and snatched a quick kiss. "You'll win. I don't have any doubt at all. It's only a matter of when. Now talk to me." She caught his hand in hers and started walking again. "What has Cole said or done this time?"

He couldn't bring himself to tell her, couldn't risk seeing that starry-eyed warmth cool into the look he'd seen after his night out with Cole. "He was just giving me race advice," Jamie offered evasively. "I'm not sure I want to take it."

She shrugged. "Then don't."

If only it were that easy. But ever since their talk, Cole would catch his eye and give him a man-to-man nod of approval, almost as though putting Bad into the wall were a done deal. As much as Jamie wanted to help his mother, he also wanted Bad Boyce's respect, as well as the respect of the racing community. There was only one way to get that. He'd have to earn it. And putting a teammate into the wall wouldn't help him accomplish that goal.

"I have an idea, if you think it would help," Stephanie offered diffidently. "Why don't you ask yourself what your father would do about whatever's bothering you?"

It wasn't a bad suggestion. And it didn't take much thought. His father would do whatever it took to protect his mother. Of course, that didn't explain why his dad had put her in this predicament in the first place. But maybe his illness had prevented him from realizing how much trouble his decision would generate.

"Everyone keeps asking about the jinx," he mentioned, deliberately changing the subject.

To his relief, the comment worked in redirecting her focus. "Weren't you listening earlier? I've told you there is no jinx. Not unless you believe there is." She tilted her head to one side. A smile flirted with her mouth, making him long for another kiss. "Do you think you're jinxed?"

"I'm trying not to…" he began. He broke off and shook his head. "No. There is no jinx."

She rewarded him with another swift kiss, and in that moment all was right with his world again. "You'll see. You're going to do fine."

He would do well. He knew it on an instinctive level. He also knew what he'd have to do in order to protect his mother. When the time came, he wouldn't shy away from it.

LUCAS HAD ALWAYS enjoyed the uniqueness of Bristol's short track with its dips and ridges. He liked the aggressiveness needed to get ahead and stay ahead. He liked the blistering speeds they managed to attain, even on a half-mile track. The constant turns and traffic, combined with that speed required total focus from the driver.

The bumping and banging reminded him of his dirt track days, especially when he was on the giving end rather than the receiving. Most of all, he appreciated the enthusiasm of the fans. Their mountaintop seats rose all around like a Roman arena, while their shouts joined with engine roar to make Bristol one of the loudest venues they attended.

There was no place like Bristol.

During the first half of the race, Lucas concentrated on staying on the lead lap, wrestling to keep the car from skating up the steep banking. "If it weren't for all these cautions, we'd be in serious trouble, Dip," he reported to his crew chief. "The handling's been off since they dropped the green."

"It's the cold front that's dropped down. We were thinking warm and instead it's colder than a witch's—"

"Careful," Lucas broke in. "First one who gets caught on a language violation is going to pay the penalty, personally."

Dipstick laughed. "How about…colder than a witch's bumpers."

"That's low, Dip." Time to get down to business. "Let's get the setup figured out. I want a Thunder Valley win."

The next hundred laps showed a steady improvement, with Dipstick working his usual magic. On lap 420 Lucas slid under Jamie and into the top ten, just behind Cole. He was going to do it, he decided. He could feel it, that bone-deep certainty that this one was within reach. After two decades racing, he'd learned to recognize and trust the instinct that told him he had a car capable of getting him to the checkered flag ahead of the rest of the field. It rarely steered him wrong.

He keyed his mike. "Start the betting pool," he ordered Dip. The phrase was one he'd used for years to signal that he was not only going for it, but was as close to positive as a driver could be that he had a shot at a win.

"Yahoo! See you in Victory Lane," Dipstick howled.

When the hit came, it totally blindsided him.

KELLIE ESCAPED the war wagon and ran flat out for the infield care center. She reached it almost at the same time as the ambulance carrying Lucas. The wait for the doctor to examine him seemed to take forever, and Kellie noticed that her heart rate barely calmed while she paced. It was a minor hit, she reassured herself. No reason to be scared. Outside the medical building she heard the roar of engines reverberating around the speedway, signaling that the race was underway once again.

Finally, the door opened and Lucas emerged. After a beat she started to breathe again. He paused in the process of fastening his uniform when he saw her. "What are you doing here?"

She struggled to recover her usual calm. "That was a nasty hit. I was concerned."

He dismissed the comment with a casual shrug. "You should be watching your other drivers, not here with me."

She ignored the comment. "Are you okay?"

"I've taken worse." He lifted an eyebrow. "What's going on, Kellie? I can understand your rushing to Jamie's side. But you and I don't have that sort of relationship."

"I always check on Cole after a wreck," she explained evasively.

"That was when you only had one driver and Jinx was still alive to cover the pits and garage." He folded his arms across his chest. "Look, Kellie, I'm flattered. But spill it. What am I missing?"

Truth time. She eyed him anxiously, not certain how he'd take this next part. "I think it was Jamie who took you out."

Lucas released his breath on a short laugh. "That's rich. Taken out by my own teammate." He thrust a hand through his damp hair, schooling his expression to patience. "Let me hear it. What happened? Is he hurt?"

"No. He's fine. His car has some front end damage they'll have to bang out."

"But—"

She hesitated. "But, it looked like he moved you."

Lucas stared in disbelief. "The kid hit me on purpose?"

"I don't know. I haven't had a conversation with ￼aps or Lucky about it, yet. But…" She blew out her ￼eath. "Yeah, it looked deliberate from where I was ￼ing." She started pacing again, aware even as she did ￼w much it gave away.

￼ bit out another laugh. "Cocky. I like that. Of c￼￼e, I'd like it better if it had been someone else. But it ￼￼d that the kid isn't intimidated by anyone."

￼t even Bad Boyce?"

￼rin faded. "Oh, he'll be intimidated by me. You can ￼￼t on it."

"￼￼s—"

H￼ ￼ok his head. "Don't defend him. I'll review the tapes ￼ if I agree with your assessment, Jamie and I will d￼ ￼ith it, man-to-man. I'm not going to have you interfe￼ ￼ and your son wouldn't appreciate having his mother ￼' A sardonic light crept into the blackness of his eye￼ ￼on't worry, momma. I'll go gentle on the boy."

"He'￼ ￼ a boy." Did Lucas catch the hint of sorrow behind t￼ ￼ealization? Based on the amused slant to his mouth, he probably did. "Okay, fine. You deal with it. I'll stay out."

"I'm glad you agree," he said drily.

She decided her best option was to ignore the comment. "You'll take a hit in the points, but it shouldn't knock you out of the top twelve."

He waved that off with a surprising lack of concern. "Next week's Martinsville. I'll pick some up there." He shot her a wry look. "Assuming your son doesn't decide to take me out again."

TWO SHORT TRACK RACES and two unfortunate wrecks in a row for Lucas had Kellie wondering whether the jinx wasn't contagious. The heaviness in the pit of her stomach told her this didn't have anything to do with a jinx, and it was something she would have to deal with sooner or later. Sooner, it appeared, as she caught sight of a visibly angry Lucas storming toward Jamie, who suddenly looked like a little boy playing dress-up in his daddy's racing uniform.

Kellie quickened her pace through their Charlotte shop in order to reach her drivers before things turned ugly. "Boys," she called, letting them know that she was there, and ready to jump in, if necessary.

Lucas's focus never shifted from Jamie. "I want to know what happened," he demanded. "Did you hit me on purpose?"

Kellie tried again. "Why don't we go to my office and—"

Lucas cut her off without compunction. "Forget it.

We do this here. In the garage where it belongs." His gaze switched back to Jamie. "Well? First Bristol and now Martinsville. Explain how you just happened to get into the back of my bumper two straight weeks in a row."

"It was just short track racing," Jamie claimed.

"I watched the videos. NASCAR watched the videos. And then they hauled your backside into the trailer, along with mine." Lucas folded his arms across his chest. "I don't like having my backside hauled into that trailer. Do you?"

The teen fixed his gaze on his sneakers and kept them there. "No."

"This was your sixth race in the NASCAR NEXTEL Cup Series. That means you've wrecked me in one third of the races you've run to date. I don't particularly like those odds."

Heat blossomed up Jamie's neck and turned his face a brilliant shade of red. "I'm sorry, Bad."

"I have two questions for you. I don't care what you've told everyone else, I want the truth. First, are you going to keep wrecking me?"

Jamie shook his head. "It was an accident."

"And second—you sure it was an accident?"

"I—" Jamie's gaze darted to Lucas and then back to his sneakers again. "It was an accident."

"Oh, Jamie," Kellie whispered in dismay. "Do you think we can't tell when you're lying? We only have to take one look at your expression to know. What's gotten into you?"

Jamie lifted his head, sheer misery reflected in his

face. He turned to Lucas. "I didn't hit you on purpose this last time," he said. "I know the videos make it look like I did, but I swear it's not true."

Lucas's mouth tightened. "But you did at Bristol."

Jamie nodded. "Yes."

"Why?"

The teen's hands balled into fists. "I don't want you to win the NASCAR Championship. I don't want you taking HRI away from my mother and firing her or something." A hint of belligerent anger crept into his voice. "I won't work for you. Not without her."

Kellie could see the effort it took Lucas to moderate his voice and keep his anger from lashing out at her son. "You're not going to be working for anyone much longer if you keep pulling this sort of stunt."

Lucas turned to confront Jamie's crew chief. "You in on this?"

Lucky forked his hand through his hair, his fingers revealing a notable tremor. "Of course not."

Lucas wasn't buying it. "You're either lying or drunk," he retorted. "Either way, you just called your last race. Pack your gear."

Kellie opened her mouth to object. One look at Lucas had her closing it again. Lucky glared at her. "You gonna let him do this? You gonna let him fire me after all the years we've worked together?"

She took a deep breath and steeled herself for one of the hardest jobs in the business—to fire an employee she genuinely liked and respected. "You're drinking again, Lucky. I can't have that. More importantly, I can't take that sort of risk with Jamie. And I guarantee you, Jinx wouldn't have either."

"He'd never have fired me!"

"Yes, he would have." Compassion spilled over into her words. "He'd have hated the necessity. But he'd have done it, anyway. Darn it, Lucky, he'd have fired you for the drinking alone. If he'd thought for one minute you'd been involved in deliberately taking out a teammate—"

"Check the audio, if you want," Lucky insisted. "I wasn't a party to it."

Jamie came to his rescue, his voice meek and eyes downcast. "It's true. Lucky didn't have anything to do with it. It was my decision and mine alone." As he spoke he looked up and Kellie heard her little boy's voice gain the resolve of a man's.

Kellie spoke to Jamie, but directed her final point toward Lucky. "You're old enough to know that alcohol abuse creates problems for the team and safety concerns for the drivers. I won't allow this to go on any longer."

A mix of surprise and disgust bled into Lucky's voice. "If Jinx were still alive, he'd have thrown the lot of you off the Hammond property before he'd have let me go." He swiveled to confront Lucas. "As for you, Boyce, I hope you enjoy your legacy as the man who drove Hammond racing into the ground."

"Oh, trust me, I will," Lucas retorted. The instant Lucky stormed off, he turned his attention to Jamie. "Whose idea was it to take me out? Yours? Or did someone else put you up to it?"

"It was my idea."

He was lying again and Kellie suspected she knew why. He was protecting someone and it didn't take much thought for her to figure out who. Cole had approached her and suggested just such a solution. The idea that the older driver might have put her son up to this had her so angry, she could barely contain it. To her relief, if Lucas picked up on Jamie's ruse or her fury, he didn't let on.

"Would you mind if I spoke to my son for a minute?" she asked in a tight voice.

"Sure." Lucas planted his fists on his hips. "Right after we decide on what sort of payback my team and I can expect."

"What do you mean?" Kellie asked warily.

"I mean there have to be consequences. I think it's only fair that I decide what those consequences should be."

More than anything she wanted to argue. But with Jamie standing there, listening on in horror, she needed to play this carefully. "What do you have in mind?"

Lucas offered a sharklike grin. "I suggest that between now and the Charlotte race, Jamie plays wrench monkey for my team. They want a tool cleaned, he cleans it. They want something taken apart or put back together, he does it. They want food, he fetches. Anything, anytime, no arguments, no discussion, no complaints."

Actually, it wasn't a bad idea. "I agree," she approved without hesitation.

"Mom!"

She rounded on her son. "That's Mrs. Hammond to

you. Go to my office. I'll deal with you as soon as I have a private word with Lucas." She waited until Jamie had left the garage before speaking again. "I'm sorry. I had no idea this was going on and I should have. It won't happen again."

"No, it won't. Hell, Kellie, I didn't expect flowers and candy from the HRI staff when I joined on, but this is ridiculous. NASCAR would have a field day over it, not to mention the media."

She didn't bother to conceal her alarm. "Lucas, I will talk to Jamie, he will serve your sentence and this will be taken care of, but I need your word that this incident doesn't leave the garage."

"Guess that would be the final straw where Food Basket is concerned." He debated for an entire gut-wrenching two minutes before inclining his head. "Leo Farmer's had enough grief over some of Jamie's stunts without adding any more fuel to the fire."

She lowered her voice and stepped closer. "Just as I can't have Lucky's behavior endangering my drivers, I need a business partner I can trust, not one I have to watch every minute."

"That goes both ways." Anger still rippled beneath the surface, but she could tell he'd regained control of it. "Let's not forget who got hit here. I'd be well within my rights to report all of this."

"If this gets out it will hurt you every bit as much as it hurts me. Worse, it could cause long-term damage to HRI."

"Which is the main reason I'm not pursuing this any further."

The sheer relief of his comment left her light-headed. "Then you agree? This incident won't leave the garage?

"This time. If I can trust you to end this here, you can trust me to keep this in-house."

"Thank you."

She didn't give him an opportunity to add any more conditions to his agreement, but headed for her office, determined to get to the bottom of this whole sorry mess. She didn't give Jamie any time to prepare his defenses. Sweeping into the office, she slammed the door behind her. She snatched up her phone and punched in her assistant's extension.

"Get Cole in here now," she ordered, then turned on Jamie. "Let me warn you right now that if you lie to me again, you will no longer be driving for HRI. So don't even try to play me. Whatever clever little fabrications you've been working on over the past five minutes, or whatever Cole might have told you to say isn't going to work. Do we understand each other?"

"Yes, ma'am."

"Give it to me straight. Cole approached you at some point before Bristol and told you to take out Lucas, didn't he?"

"Not in so many words."

"But he implied as much."

"He said it would be best for HRI and for you," Jamie admitted miserably. "I was trying to protect you, Mom. If Bad wins the championship, he could take

HRI away from you. What was I supposed to do? Just let him?" He shook his head, his jaw taking on an all-too-familiar jut. "No way am I going to do that. With Dad gone, it's my job to look after you."

Before she had a chance to respond, a knock sounded at the door and Cole walked in, offering a broad smile. One look at Jamie's wretched expression, as well as Kellie's undisguised fury, had his smile fading. "Uh-oh. Busted." He gave Jamie an understanding shrug. "I don't blame you. I know you wouldn't have ratted me out unless they beat it out of you."

"I'm sorry, Cole."

"Don't you *dare* apologize to him," Kellie bit out. She turned on Cole. "And how could you use my son like that? Have you completely lost your mind?"

He turned wide, ingenuous eyes in her direction. "Come on, Kellie. I was only doing what you wanted."

"What *I* wanted, or what *you* wanted? And while we're on the subject, you didn't actually do anything, did you? You were too careful for that." She stabbed a finger in Jamie's direction. "Instead you used Jamie as your patsy, you son of a—" She broke off before the words could be uttered.

"Look, it wasn't like that. At least, not exactly."

The breath shuddered from her lungs as the full weight of the "could have beens" hit her. She thrust her hair from her face with trembling hands. "Dear God, Cole. He could have lost his ride. He still might if Food Basket gets wind of this—or of the fact that it was deliberate. They could pull out. As it is, he's lost the respect of other drivers who are publicly calling him cocky and arrogant. And he now has NASCAR watching his every move. One more infraction and he's in serious trouble. He's only eighteen. And in one stupid move, he's put his entire future in jeopardy. Not yours. His." She paced off some of her fury. "Though allow me to assure you you're not off the hook, either. I'm warning you. One more false move on your part and I'll fire you."

The words had no sooner left her mouth when her office door crashed open. Lucas stood there. The instant he spotted Cole, he charged across the room. Catching him by the throat, Lucas slammed Cole against the wall.

CHAPTER NINE

"Did you think I wouldn't find out? Did you think someone wouldn't give you up? You're not that popular, Whaling. At least, not in the garage. Maybe you should spend less time mugging for the cameras and more time bonding with your men."

"Get the hell off me!" Cole shoved at Lucas, but couldn't break his hold. "I don't know what you're talking about."

"I'm talking about convincing the kid to wreck me. I'm talking about interfering where you don't belong because you're hoping to scoop up a piece of HRI for yourself by romancing it out from under your boss."

"That's enough!" Kellie couldn't remember the last time she'd been this angry. Or scared. The two men broke apart, though she knew they'd be battling it out again at the least provocation. "Jamie, head down to Lucas's shop. Now. I don't care what they want you to do, or how dirty the job, you're to do it. Are we clear?"

"Yes, ma'am." He eyed the two men with clear-cut uncertainty. "Maybe I should wait a minute or two before leaving."

"Don't you worry about me." She scrutinized the

combatants with grim intent. "I'm more than capable of taking care of this little problem."

The instant the door closed behind Jamie, Lucas planted a fist in Cole's face, knocking him to the ground. He stood over him, the breath hissing between his teeth. "Get up again, you scum-sucking piece of snake turd. Get up, so I can knock you down again."

"It was a joke," Cole claimed desperately. "A joke that got out of hand."

"You suppose NASCAR will see it that way? Why don't we give them a quick call and find out?"

"Nobody is calling NASCAR. This stays in-house, as agreed," Kellie snapped. "Lucas, back off. You hit him again and I'm calling security. Then you can deal with your own morals clause with Wolf Sportsman."

Lucas stood there for endless seconds, no doubt weighing his options. After a full minute, he shot her a single smoldering glare, and fell back a step. It was just far enough to appear as though he were falling in line, while still close enough to take Cole on if the other man so much as twitched.

"Were you in on it, too?" Lucas demanded of her.

The fact that he needed to ask the question hurt more than she thought possible. "You should know the answer to that without having to ask. If I'd had any idea that Cole intended to involve Jamie in this, I'd have fired him on the spot." She cut her gaze to the other man. "I still might."

"Did you know Whaling planned to take me out?" Lucas pressed. She hesitated, a hesitation that cost her dearly. Fury flared anew. "Son of a bitch! You did know."

She kept her eyes trained on him, forcing herself to remain as direct and unguarded as possible. "Cole mentioned putting his bumper to you as a way to keep you from gaining controlling interest in HRI. I told him in no uncertain terms that he wasn't to interfere in any way, shape, or form."

"She's telling the truth," Cole stated wearily.

"Shut up, Whaling. When I want your opinion I'll beat it out of you." He took a single step in Kellie's direction, a step that had Cole shooting to his feet.

"Leave her out of this," Cole warned. "You want to lay into me, have at it. At least I deserve it. But if you so much as touch her, I'll take you apart."

"How noble."

"You want the truth? You want to know why I did it? Fine." Tension filled the other driver, along with a painful indignation. "I saw you and Kellie kissing outside of Jamie's hospital room after Daytona. I didn't like it. Fact is, I still don't like it. Jinx had only been gone a few weeks at that point. So, I used Jamie to even the score. Consider it divine retribution, since I'm sure Jinx would have approved wholeheartedly of what I did."

That caught Lucas's attention. "Had her pegged for yourself, did you?"

"You do both realize I'm still standing here," Kellie broke in. She was determined to take charge again. "I'm not a bone to be fought over and I refuse to be treated like one. Cole."

The driver spared her a swift glance. His left eye

was already swelling and the sight of it had her mouth compressing. "You understand why I did it, don't you?" he asked.

"Not even a little. Get some ice on that eye before the doctor has you sidelined at Texas. I'll discuss disciplinary action with Lucas and let you know the consequences. Until then I suggest you get yourself under control. Am I clear?"

His jaw worked for a moment before he gave an abrupt nod. "Crystal, boss."

"Get out of here."

He didn't wait for a second invitation, but crossed the width of her office and exited. Kellie couldn't help but notice that he gave Lucas a wide berth. As soon as they were alone, she returned her attention to her partner. "Now you can say whatever you need to."

"Assuming I believe that you weren't directly involved in what happened, you knew there was a possibility that Cole would try something. You should have warned me. And even if you didn't think he'd use Jamie to take me out, that possibility occurred to you after what happened at Bristol, didn't it?"

"Yes, but you watched the video replay and didn't see anything." Honesty forced her to concede, "But you're right. I should have told you what Cole said. At the time, you'd just joined HRI and I didn't want to create any dissension between you and Cole."

"I'll say it again, Kellie. You've taken on too much. You're stretched too thin to stay on top of everything that's happening."

She refused to accept that. "No, the real problem is we're not working as a team and I can't trust any of you. I'm having to babysit my drivers, as well as run a three-team racing organization."

Lucas took a minute to consider that before nodding in agreement. "Fair enough." He shot her a glance from beneath furrowed eyebrows. "You do realize this has to change. We have to find a way to all work together instead of everyone running around half-cocked."

She folded her arms across her chest. "I'm listening. What do you suggest?"

"I suggest that for the good of HRI, you and I join forces." He shifted closer and lowered his voice, which only gave his words added impact. "On all fronts."

She turned that one over, not sure she'd heard him right. "That sounds remarkably like a proposition."

He nodded. "You have excellent hearing." Before she could gather her wits enough to react, he continued. "Now, shall we discuss Cole and how you intend to handle that problem?"

It took a second to switch gears. "I intend to fine him and put him on probation. According to our contract, this was a firing offense and it's my choice whether I stick a price tag on his actions or kick him to the curb. I'd rather not replace him at this point in the season." She grimaced. "I'd rather not replace him at all. For all his flaws, he's still an outstanding driver, not to mention that the fans are crazy about him. All in all, it makes him a valuable addition to HRI. That said, I can't have one of my drivers deliberately taking out another."

"Make the fine stiff enough to hurt and I can live with it."

Residual anger still clung to him and she attempted to soothe it. "You're only one spot out of twelfth. There's still plenty of time to make up the difference."

"Oh, I'll make it up." His eyes were as hard as diamonds. "All this did was jack with me a bit. Tends to make me more ornery. You can't shake a wolf by kicking him, and Cole's going to find that out if he comes after me again." He took one final step closer. "Now that we've resolved our business issues, I suggest we discuss our personal ones."

Alarmed, she shook her head. "I've told you before, we don't have any personal issues."

"If that were true, Whaling wouldn't have gone after me. He sees what you refuse to." Determination settled into his expression. "You want me."

"No—"

Lucas silenced her with one simple touch. He skimmed his hand along the curve of her cheek, just as he had all those weeks ago when he'd first arrived at HRI and she'd shown him his office. The effect was identical. Desire swept through her with an intensity that stole her breath. She didn't have a hope of concealing her reaction from him. Sure enough, a smile tugged at the corner of his mouth and his eyes softened.

"If it makes you feel any better, it's the same for me. I want you, Kellie." He paused a beat, then added pointedly, "I also intend to have you."

She shivered. "That's not going to happen."

"Time will tell."

He left the office then, and she sank into her seat. Deep inside, she couldn't help but wonder. If Lucas made a play for her, she wanted to believe she could resist him. But considering she'd never been able to before this, chances were excellent that he was right. Before long, he'd follow through on his promise, and she doubted she was capable of stopping him.

"THE RACING WORLD is abuzz over the latest coming from HRI. Jinx Junior's family curse has struck two weeks in a row, both times taking out his teammate and last year's NASCAR NEXTEL Cup Champion, Lucas 'Bad' Boyce. The wreck resulted in HRI owner Kellie Hammond, Lucas Boyce and Jamie Hammond, as well as their respective crew chiefs, being invited to the NASCAR trailer to meet with the powers-that-be for a serious discussion, no doubt regarding race track etiquette.

"When asked for a comment, Bad is reported to have said, 'Jamie and I have discussed the matter and will be working closely together to resolve it.' Rumors coming from both camps indicate that there might have been more than words exchanged.

"Fellow teammate Cole Whaling confirmed the suggestion of in-house dissension. 'Boyce is just annoyed because these past two weeks he's been on the receiving end of a bumper for a change. No one else would dare move The Big Bad out of the way. I've got to hand it to the kid. He's got chops.'

"So far no comment from Jinx Junior or HRI owner

Kellie Hammond. As soon as we hear what was said behind closed doors—and our understanding is that it was an earful—you'll hear. And one of our first questions will be…who gave Cole that impressive shiner he's sporting? Stay tuned, race fans!"

KELLIE STOOD shoulder-to-shoulder with her father, staring through the bank of windows overlooking the shops a full story beneath them. Jamie, Lucas and his team were working on the cars and had been for eight hours straight. She'd never seen her son look so filthy or so exhausted—or so happy.

Until a few hours ago the entire crew had taken great delight in torturing the teenager with the worst chores they could dream up. And while one part of her had fretted over the treatment of her son, the other part had taken pride in his tenacity, good humor and willingness to take whatever garbage they chose to dish out.

When she'd last peeked down at them an hour or so ago, she'd noticed a change in attitude. Instead of treating Jamie like something that had crawled out of some slimy bog, they'd begun to accept him as one of the team. Even better, several of the mechanics had switched to teaching mode and were actively explaining the hows and whys of what they were doing. And though Jamie had spent his entire life with his head buried under the hood of a car, he soaked up each and every pointer with undisguised enthusiasm.

Best of all was the interaction between Jamie and Lucas. Tension had radiated between them earlier. That, too, had changed. Now they were joking together and acting as though there'd never been a disagreeable word between them.

"I was a little worried," Darrell admitted, watching the byplay between the two.

"Me, too," Kellie confessed.

"I wasn't sure how those two would shake down. I have to admit, I'm relieved to see them getting on so well." He leaned his forearm against the glass as he watched his grandson. "When are you going to tell them?"

"Tell them…what?" she asked warily.

"Tell them that they're father and son."

Kellie's breath caught in an audible gasp. "What are you talking about? He's Jinx's son, not—"

"Don't." Just that one word. So soft. So gentle. So implacable. "Don't lie to your father. It isn't right. It wasn't right eighteen years ago and it isn't now."

She closed her eyes and gave in to the inevitable. "When did you find out? Did Jinx tell you?"

"We never spoke of it." A hint of regret rippled through her father's comment. "Alluded to it, the way men do. Wish things could have been different. Proud to have Jamie for a son. That sort of thing."

"If Jinx didn't tell you, then how did you know?"

He turned his head and stared at her with such a wealth of pain that she flinched. "Little girl, do you really think I wouldn't have known if you'd been sneaking out with my driver? Do you think I wouldn't have been the first to knock a few teeth down Jinx's throat if I'd ever suspected he'd messed with my baby?"

"I was afraid to tell you," she whispered.

"And that hurts most of all." He pulled her into his arms, resting his chin on the top of her head. "I wanted to think that you could have come to me for anything. That you knew I would stand by you and take care of you."

She shook her head. "I knew you'd have stood by me. But you'd have been so disappointed in me."

"Maybe a bit. But I'd have gotten over it soon enough." She could hear his smile reflected in his voice. "Especially the minute I set eyes on my grandbaby. 'Course then I'd have taken my shotgun and turned the hurting end on young Boyce. And that, I suspect, is the real reason you didn't tell me."

She couldn't deny it. "Sounds about right."

"You were so young."

She pulled back, offering him a watery smile. "And so foolish."

"Did you love him?"

"I thought I did."

A hint of anger drifted through Darrell's blue eyes. "But he didn't love you."

She shook her head. "No, he didn't. He was focused on his career." She planted a kiss on her father's cheek. "It wasn't his fault, Paps. At least, not much."

"Which takes us back to my original question… When are you going to tell those two the truth?"

Kellie caught her lower lip between her teeth. "Do you really think I should?"

"They both deserve to know."

"But Jinx—"

"Was the most honest, up-front man I ever met. I'm surprised he didn't insist you tell Lucas long ago."

"He did," she admitted. "I flat-out refused to hear it."

"And because you did, he went to Lucas and sold him a big chunk of HRI. Why do you suppose that was, Kellie?" He didn't wait for her answer. "You know why. It was because he wanted to bring the three of you together. It was one of his last acts, a silent plea that you do the right thing."

She couldn't hold her tears at bay any longer. "I know," she said brokenly. "But how do I tell them after all these years?"

"It won't be easy. But it has to be done."

"I'm afraid I'll lose Jamie when he finds out." And Lucas? a tiny voice whispered. She doubted he'd take her subterfuge well. Not after what he perceived as her involvement in Cole's scheme.

"It'll be tough on the boy, but he'll survive."

"If Jamie finds out he's not Jinx's son, it might have a serious impact on his racing. He's shaky enough as it is." She shook her head. "I can't take the risk right now. I'll tell them both after the season ends. That way they'll have the off-season to deal with it."

"It's your choice," Darrell conceded. "I just hope your decision doesn't backfire on you."

She shivered, praying her father's words weren't prophetic, but on a purely visceral level, she suspected they were.

"So what do you think?"

Kellie checked her stopwatch and nodded in agreement. "He just went to the top of the qualifying board. Jamie's improvement is amazing." She smiled up at Lucas. "A lot of this is thanks to you. You realize that, don't you?"

He shook his head. "It's Jamie behind that steering wheel."

"But it's you who's helped him with his self-confidence. To ignore the 'Jinx Junior' label and simply race. He's always had phenomenal focus. But being under this sort of scrutiny would shake even a seasoned driver."

"He's a quick study." Lucas watched Jamie come around again and take the checkered flag to signal the end of his Richmond qualifying lap. "I have to admit I was wrong. I didn't think he had the chops to jump right into the NASCAR NEXTEL Cup Series. But this past month he's proven he was born to hold a wheel. The kid's a natural."

Kellie grinned. The bond that had formed between Lucas and Jamie thrilled her beyond words. Watching them together she wondered how anyone could mistake their relationship. Despite the difference in their hair and eye color, their builds were identical. So was the way they moved, along with the level of their focus and intensity. But most telling of all was that slow smile they shared.

Soon. She'd have to tell them the truth soon. Just not yet. Right now she wanted to savor the budding relationship she was enjoying with Lucas without the emotional turmoil that would come once she revealed the truth.

Cole hit the track next and she caught the slight compression of Lucas's mouth. "He's trying," she said in a low voice. "He hasn't caused any more trouble."

"Yet."

"He's become the odd man out over the past four weeks. That's a pretty steep punishment for a man like Cole," she said, trying to reason with Lucas. "Even more of a punishment than anything NASCAR or HRI could impose on him."

He folded his arms across his chest. "Don't kid yourself, Kellie. Cole's riding high after that win at Talladega. Holding at second in the points race hasn't hurt, either."

"I don't care what's caused the change, so long as it stays."

Lucas gave her a look of undisguised amusement. "It'll last as long as he keeps winning and as long as I remain behind him in the points. When that changes, so will he. Face facts, partner. He's biding his time."

She checked her stopwatch as an excuse to escape the hold of those all-too-discerning eyes. How was it possible after all this time that he could still fluster her so badly? "The bottom line is that Cole's behaving. Right now, I'll take whatever I can get in that regard."

Lucas crowded close under the pretext of checking the time she'd recorded. "And when he stops trying?"

"We'll deal with that when it happens."

He didn't move away as she'd expected and she

worked to conceal the slight tremble of hands and voice and heart that occurred whenever he came near. These were stolen minutes, moments of forbidden pleasure, when she could imagine how her life might have been if she and Lucas had been in different places when they'd first met. If he'd been a few years further along in his career. If she'd been a few years older. If their love affair could have had a chance to grow and develop instead of their experiencing that one fleeting night before going their separate ways. But those changes would have meant she'd never have had Jamie.

She couldn't imagine life without her son. He'd been a joy to her, despite the shock of her unexpected pregnancy. No. She wouldn't change anything, not even if it meant she'd have had a chance of a long-term relationship with Lucas.

He touched her hand, caught the slight tremor and gathered it up within the strength of his hold. "What's wrong?"

"Nothing." She shook her head more adamantly than the moment called for. "Sorry. Got lost in my thoughts."

"Sad thoughts." His hold gentled. "Jinx?"

Her throat tightened, preventing her from speaking the lie. She couldn't even bring herself to nod in order to duck the question. She'd told so many lies and half-truths, was so tired of the subterfuge. What would happen if she turned to him, turned and looked into those green eyes and told him the truth? How would he react?

It didn't take any thought. He'd despise her. And so would her son.

"It's almost time for you to qualify," she warned, switching to a brisk "boss" mode. "Go make nice to the cameras and tell them how you plan to win this thing Saturday night."

"Kellie—"

She refused to look at him, to acknowledge how badly she wanted to turn into his arms and say to hell with the cameras all around them. To forget about Cole and Jamie and everyone else scrutinizing them with such keen, predatory interest. To grab hold of Lucas and inhale him. To surrender to the desire that underscored every word and thought and touch. But she couldn't. She didn't dare.

"Step back, Lucas. There are cameras on us."

"Let them watch," came his hard reply. "I don't give a damn."

"HRI has stirred up enough controversy without adding to it."

"It's coming, Kellie. Deny it all you want. But the day is coming when you won't turn away from me."

She adjusted her wraparound sunglasses. She'd never before been as grateful for them as she was in this moment. "Good luck with your lap."

"That's it?"

She nodded, fixing her gaze on anything and everything but the man at her side. "That's it."

"But you'll be watching me." He was close. So close she could feel the warmth of his breath on her cheek. "You'll be watching me every inch of the way, won't you?" He didn't wait for her response, but started down pit road past the line of cars waiting for their chance to qualify.

"I've always been watching," she whispered.

FROM THE MOMENT Jamie drove onto Richmond's three-quarter-mile asphalt track, he felt as though he'd come home. He couldn't explain it, he just knew at a gut-deep level that Richmond was his track. Every driving instinct he possessed kicked into high gear, whispering to him that he could win here.

"That's definitely a pole effort," Paps informed him after Jamie had completed all his post-qualifying duties. "That should give a few of your fans a thrill."

"Really?" Jamie grinned. "You really think I have a shot at the pole?"

"More than a shot, kid." Cole came up and gave him a congratulatory slap on the back that reminded Jamie of how it had been between them before Bristol and Martinsville. "You don't get the pole, I'll eat my lugnuts. Hell, you don't get the pole by a full tenth of a second, I'll eat my lugnuts and my wheels."

Jamie's cell phone rang as Cole headed for his hauler. After checking the number, he hastened to answer it. "Did you see? Were you watching?"

"Are you kidding?" Stephanie crowed. "Wait, wait! They're announcing it now. You got it, Jamie! You got the pole."

He whirled around to check with his grandfather, who gave him the thumbs-up, followed by a broad, proud grin. "I only have a second to talk before the reporters find me. You're coming Saturday, aren't you?"

"Of course I am. I wouldn't miss your first pole for the world."

"Stephanie, I—"

"Jinx! Jinx Junior!"

"Stephanie? I have to go. They're coming for me. I just wanted you to know—"

"I do know. I'll see you on Saturday. And Jamie? Don't let them get to you. You're not a jinx."

Jamie glanced over his shoulder and released his breath in a sigh. As usual, she read him like a book. Only one cloud continued to shadow the sunny blue of his sky. Despite having had three exemplary racing weeks, the press continued to yammer on about "Jinx Junior," waiting breathlessly for the jinx to strike again. It didn't matter how often he explained that everyone had the occasional run of bad luck, some of the more sensationalist reporters were determined to attribute every ill-timed pit stop or unsuccessful car setup or badly executed pass to the Hammond Jinx.

If it hadn't been for Lucas's calm dismissal of the entire situation, Jamie suspected he'd have been a nervous wreck. Instead, he'd been given direction, direction he'd badly needed since his father's illness and death. Jamie set his jaw. Today he'd show them all. Today he'd proven that his parents' decision to put him in the legendary Number 56 car hadn't been a mistake.

Saturday night came in a whirlwind of publicity and interviews. Through it all, he greeted the reporters with a friendly smile, answering every last question in a calm, confident manner. He was in this for the long haul and that meant learning to handle every aspect of the business, not just the driving.

Stephanie kept her distance whenever the press was around. Shortly before the start of the race he made a point of taking her into his hauler so he could have a few private words with her out of the public eye. More than anything he wanted to collect a kiss for good luck. Relieved to find they had the place to themselves, he locked them in the room he'd reserved for his own use.

"I know your dad would have a fit if he found out we were here like this." Out of habit, he groped for the locket he still wore each time he raced. "But tonight's special."

"I know you're going to do well. I feel it in my bones." She pressed a hand to his, their fingers joining over the small mound her locket made through his uniform. "You feel it, too, don't you?"

He nodded. "It's going to go well tonight."

There was a moment of silent awareness. And then he pulled her into his arms and kissed her. This time it wasn't a quick, tentative brush of lips. This time he let her know how he felt. How much she meant to him.

He heard the tiny hitch in her breathing that signaled her surprise. Then her hands clutched at his shoulders before sliding around his neck to cling to him. She was so soft, so fragile, in comparison to him. So giving. He wanted to love her. To protect her. To have her in his life every moment of every day and keep her there.

His kiss hardened, grew more demanding. He half

expected her to pull back. But she didn't. Instead, she returned kiss for kiss. She seemed to melt into him, and his reaction was instantaneous. If they'd been anywhere but locked in his hauler only moments before driver introductions, he'd have allowed her response to carry them further, possibly to a natural conclusion. But he couldn't.

He pulled back as gently as he could. "Stephanie," he whispered. "We can't."

She smiled up at him, her dark eyes luminous, her lips ripe and swollen from his kisses. "I wish we could."

"Me, too."

"Really? Then why are you frowning?" She tilted her head to one side, her discernment never ceasing to surprise him. "It isn't just the timing, is it?"

"It's my mom," he admitted in a rush.

She nodded in perfect understanding. "You're worried she might find out."

"She wouldn't be any happier than your father, that's for sure. But it's not just that." He hesitated, before confessing, "It's me. My birth. You see, Mom was a year younger than us when she had me."

Stephanie's eyes widened. "She was only seventeen? You're joking."

"She married my dad when she found out. But it wasn't—" He shrugged. "It wasn't like us. Do you know what I mean?"

She smiled again, a shy, teasing sort of smile. "No, I don't know what you mean. What's it like with us?"

He didn't hesitate. He took exquisite care to show her,

drawing out the moment, making it as special as he could. "That's us," he murmured against her mouth. "That's how it is between us. I love you, Stephanie. I know it's probably too soon to tell you. But I can't help how I feel."

"I love you, too, Jamie."

Determination solidified. "They're going to try and stop us," he warned. "They won't believe it's real or that it'll last."

"I don't care what they say or do. What we feel is real."

"Then we'll find a way to work it out." Determination filled him. "This is how we're going to do it. We're going to take it slow and easy. We'll let them get used to the idea of our being together. And I'm going to do my best both on the track and off. After a while they'll realize that the world hasn't stopped spinning just because we found each other at eighteen instead of at twenty-two or twenty-five."

"And us?" A hint of color blossomed in her cheeks. "When we want to be together?"

He cupped her face and gave her a reassuring kiss. "We wait until it's right. And when it is, we make sure we don't repeat history."

Someone banged on the door. "Driver introductions, Jamie," came Paps's voice. "Give that girl a kiss for luck and haul your butt out here before someone who can fire you finds out you're in there alone with her."

Jamie grinned. "Coming, Paps." He lowered his voice. "You heard my grandfather. I'm under orders to give you a kiss for luck."

She shot him a demure look from beneath her lashes, one belied by the distinct twinkle of amusement in her eyes. "I don't know about you, but I try never to argue with my grandfather."

He grinned down at her. "Me, neither."

"One more kiss and then I want you to win me a race."

"This is just the start," he promised. "It's only going to get better from now on."

CHAPTER TEN

"HRI IS HOT, HOT, HOT! How hot, you ask? Well, let's start with the youngest team member. Jinx Junior seems to have overcome the bad luck that dogged him at Bristol and Martinsville with his impressive second-place finish at Richmond. Following that up with a top-ten at Darlington has propelled the fan-favorite rookie into nineteenth place. Way to go, Jamie!

"When it comes to Jamie's teammates, the score so far is Cole Whaling with one win and Bad Boyce taking first place in NASCAR NEXTEL Cup's All-Star race. Granted, it won't add to his points total. But it does make his banker smile and gives Bad a full year's worth of bragging rights.

"Over the next several days, drivers prepare for the grueling six-hundred-mile race at Charlotte on Memorial Day weekend. Will Bad sweep both races? Or will his young teammate pull a Bristol on him? Will Cole continue to lead the HRI pack in points, or will last year's NASCAR NEXTEL Cup Champion relegate him to second place, once again? We'll find out the answers to all these questions when racing continues at Charlotte in just six more days!"

LUCAS WOVE BACK and forth down the backstretch of Charlotte's mile-and-a-half quad-oval track, working the heat into his tires as he and forty-two other cars streamed toward the drop of the green flag.

"Okay, guys," he informed his team. "If we can manage a repeat of last week, we'll have this bad boy in the bag."

"You want I should start the betting pool right off?" Dip drawled.

Lucas chuckled. "Let's give it a few laps. Six hundred miles is a ways to go. A lot can happen before we get anywhere close."

"Nah. All you need to do is avoid anyone stupid."

That elicited laughter all around. And then it was time for him to gather up his focus and direct it toward the early laps of the race. To organize his strategy, consider various contingencies, and, of course, race the hell out of his machine.

The wrecks were more frequent than the week before. The current points leader, Hutch Matheson, was one of the first into the wall, turned by rookie Davy Ellis. Lucas shook his head. There'd be words over that one. And if Hutch got Davy alone off-track, more than words.

"Congratulations, Bad. According to our sources, that wreck just moved you into the top twelve in points again."

Satisfaction filled him. "What do you say we stay there?"

"You're on."

And he did. It was as though Lucas were touched by magic that night and the entire team knew it, the magic rubbing off on them, as well. He loved the blistering speed. He loved the side-by-side racing. He loved how Charlotte fit his natural rhythm as a driver and how he seemed to have an instinct for knowing when and where a wreck would develop, and avoiding it. Best of all, he loved that they were able to stay on top of the adjustments the entire night.

Every pit stop was sheer poetry in motion, their times consistently the fastest of all the competitors. There'd only been a few races he'd run where it felt as though he could do no wrong. This was one of those races. During the daylight hours, he hung toward the middle of the pack. He didn't worry. His car would come to him when night fell and the track cooled. The instant it did, he started moving forward.

Three quarters of the way through the race he had his closest call. "Wreck high. Stay low," his spotter bit out. "Lower. Snake low, Bad."

He couldn't see through all the smoke. All he could go on was the voice in his ear and his own gut instinct. He slammed into the bank of smoke, cars wrecking on either side of him. He wove with the skill and precision of a surgeon, cutting between debris, cars and wrecks in progress. Shooting out the other side, he fought to breathe.

"Well, that was one hell of a ride," he announced when he finally made it through.

"Way to go, Bad!" Dipstick howled. "They'll be showing that on replays for the rest of the year."

"How many laps left?"

"Fifty laps, seventy-five miles. You ready to put this baby to bed?"

"Sure am," he confirmed. "Boys, it's time to start the betting pool."

"He's going to do it," Dipstick crowed. "I've got a feeling in my bones about this one."

So did Lucas. Lap after lap he ate through the cars between him and the checkered flag. The race had taken on a long green-flag run and final pit stops were starting. "I want four. And loosen me up a tad, I've picked up a slight chatter in the front. Let's get this last adjustment right."

They did. The change allowed him to run his favored line, his speed picking up significantly. By the final ten laps, he was in second behind the leader, Rufus McCall, and bearing down hard. With three to go, they were running nose-to-tail, driving as hard as they could into each corner. On Turn One of the last lap, Lucas used his speed coming out of the corner to power down the straightaway and flat outran McCall going into Turn Two. He dove hard into the corner and came out onto the backstretch having snatched the lead by mere inches.

If McCall were going to get him, it would be in Turns Three or Four, where the track widened into two groves. Side by side, the two of them drove hard into Turn Three. Coming off Turn Four, McCall tried to pinch Lucas as they hit the corner where the track narrowed. They skated toward the finish line, leaning on each other. But in those final couple hundred feet, McCall couldn't hang on to his car. His back end started around and Lucas shot ahead, taking the checkered flag while McCall snagged second in a flat-out spin that left him stalled in the grass in front of pit road.

Cheers erupted through his headset as Lucas rolled around the race track a final time while his fellow competitors came up alongside, giving him a wave or a light bang on the door. Jamie was one of the former, Cole the latter. But it was the one voice bubbling in his ear that made his victory complete.

"That was one of the best races I've ever seen you run, Lucas. Congratulations!"

There was undisguised admiration in Kellie's voice that had to be more than his imagination. A warmth and intimacy that went beyond partners or owner/driver. He couldn't help but wonder if anyone else interpreted it the way he had.

Even more, he wondered whether she'd admit as much the next time he kissed her.

THE PARTY WAS in full swing, lanterns strung around the huge expanse of lawn throwing a soft glow over the HRI employees who'd gathered to celebrate Lucas's dual win at Charlotte.

Kellie was pleased at what the past few weeks had wrought, the teams finally pulling together, instead of apart. Maybe it was the fact that they'd managed to bring some of their various issues into the open. Or maybe they realized that they'd be in Dover next week. And Dover would mark the halfway point in the Race for the Chase, which ended back at Richmond in early September and determined who would be among the top twelve vying for the ultimate prize.

It was time to get serious. Time to focus on what was most important—a run at the NASCAR NEXTEL Cup Championship.

Tonight, though, was an evening of celebration. The weather had cooperated, hovering in the low 70s and splashing brilliant sheets of sunshine down on them when everyone had first arrived. Now it had cooled slightly as evening set in. But most stayed warm dancing to the band she'd hired and feasting on the selection of barbecue and side dishes she'd had catered for their enjoyment.

"I can't believe you're here all alone."

The voice came from the darkness behind her, and she glanced over her shoulder not the least surprised to find Lucas there. On some intuitive level she'd sensed him, had known he'd come for her. "But, I'm not alone," she said. "You're with me."

"So I am." He offered a lazy smile and took a seat next to her at the table. "Worn out already?"

She released her breath in a soft sigh. "Isn't that what happens when you hit thirty-five? Everything starts breaking down and wearing out?"

"Considering I have four years on you, I sure as hell hope not."

She shrugged. "Then maybe it's just me."

"Or maybe you're just overdoing."

"Back to that, are we?" But her retort lacked heat. Tonight it took too much energy to work up a good mad, especially when she was in such a good mood. Besides, she was tired of fighting Lucas. There were so many other things she'd rather do with him, not one of them appropriate.

"I told you my solution to your problem." The calm reason in his voice snagged her attention where a more demanding comment wouldn't have. "Let me help."

"Are you asking or telling?" She couldn't resist the question, nor her interest in hearing his response.

He held up his hands in surrender. "Asking."

"Then, yes. I suspect I am overdoing it and could use more help. There, I've admitted it. And as long as I'm being so informative, let me also tell you that now that I've had time to consider everything that's happened over the past few months—" She broke off and shifted to face him. "I have a confession. You were right about Lucky. I didn't want to hear it because he'd been with us for so long."

"And because you're softhearted." He tucked a curl behind her ear. "That's not a bad quality. It can just get in the way when you have to make the tough decisions."

"It doesn't get in your way, does it?"

He shook his head. "Not often."

She couldn't contain her curiosity. "When has it? When has your heart ever overridden your head?"

He took so long to respond, she didn't think he would. "It's only happened three times."

"So many?" she marveled. "I'm shocked."

"You should be, considering all three times involved you."

Now she really was shocked. "I don't understand. What? When?"

He reached for her hand in the darkness, lacing their fingers together. "The first time was years ago when we made love. I knew you were trouble from the first moment I laid eyes on you. There was a little voice warning me that something was off about the whole situation. But I didn't care. That night I wanted you and nothing was going to stop me from having you."

She fought to conceal her reaction from him, and the painful longing the memory stirred. "And the second time?"

"In the hauler at Daytona. I started to kiss you, remember?"

"But we were interrupted." She was eternally grateful for the darkness that swallowed up the warmth stealing into her cheeks. "You did kiss me later," she reminded him.

"Ah, but that was different. Daytona was pure impulse. All the other times, I'd already made up my mind to take whatever I could get." He lifted her hand to his mouth and pressed a kiss into her palm. "That day in your hauler, I was running on pure emotion, not a brain cell to be found."

"All the other times we kissed, it was planned?"

She caught the flash of white from his smile. "Let's say it was my head giving permission to the more desperate parts of my anatomy. I considered my choices and made the only logical one."

"Which was?"

"To give in to my emotions." He lifted his shoulders in a shrug. "Considering I can rarely control them where you're concerned, it seemed a reasonable option."

The admission left her disconcerted, a ridiculous reaction given her age. "You…you said there was a third time. When was that?"

"Here." He tugged at her hand, drawing her closer. "Now."

She resisted the pull. "No. We can't. People will see."

"Is that your only excuse?"

The warmth of his breath caressed her face. He was so close she could almost taste him, could almost feel his lips on hers. And she wanted him. Wanted him as she'd wanted no other, ever. He'd been her first love. Her only love. He was Jamie's father. How was it possible that after all these years, after all this time apart, that she'd still have such feelings for him? It defied understanding.

"You just want an affair."

He didn't deny it. "Yes."

"I don't do affairs."

"You have with me."

The reminder hurt. "Please." She closed her eyes. "I was seventeen. Haven't I paid enough for that foolishness?"

"Shhh." He rested his forehead against hers. "It was

foolish only because of your age and expectations. But that didn't change what happened that night. It was unlike anything I've ever experienced before or since."

She shuddered at the confession. "Bridgette—"

"Was a pale imitation." His mouth brushed hers. "Maybe that's what I was to you, before you and Jinx got together. Maybe I was your pale imitation. If that's the case, I understand why you wouldn't want to go there again. Just say the word, and I'll walk away. And I won't bother you again."

She'd told so many lies, tried so hard to protect herself and Jamie. But with those few words, he'd shredded her emotions and demolished barriers she'd thought she'd built so high and strong that they'd never be breached. Maybe she'd been making a mistake all these weeks. Maybe she should take what he offered and have one more night with him. Maybe, if she made love to him again, whatever insanity they shared would finally fade and she could get on with her life.

He started to pull away, misinterpreting her silence. "Wait," she whispered.

"Be sure, Kellie. Be very sure."

"Just this one night. Just like last time."

"And then?"

"And then it'll be the way you said. We'll have it out of our systems and it'll be back to business as usual. If anything, it should be a relief. We won't have this—" Her hand fluttered. "Whatever *this* is. We won't have it between us anymore."

"Is that what you think?" A thread of amusement

drifted through his voice. "You think one night will put out the fire?"

"It's going to have to."

He started to reply, then broke off with a shrug. "Time will tell. When and where?"

"Tonight after the party breaks up." She couldn't believe she was doing this. Or that she'd waited so long. "There's a guesthouse on the opposite side of the property."

"On the edge of the woods?"

"That's the one. I'll meet you there at… Would midnight work?"

"I'll see you then."

The rest of the evening inched by, the minutes feeling like hours. Finally, the party wound down. She lingered, joking with the stragglers and thanking each and every one for all their hard work. Finally, only Paps and Jamie remained and she walked with them up to the main house. Heading for her bedroom, she freshened up before slipping outside again.

Moonlight lit her path to the guesthouse. Just as she reached the front door, Lucas stepped from the shadows and, even though she'd been expecting him, she couldn't prevent her start of surprise.

"Sorry. I didn't mean to frighten you."

"I shouldn't have been. I knew you'd be here."

She sounded strained and breathless, a fact he took note of.

"Are you having second thoughts?" Lucas asked.

"No. Yes." She started to laugh. "I guess I must be."

"We don't have to go through with this," he said, though she suspected it cost him dearly to make the offer.

"No, we don't."

Instead of moving away from him, she stepped closer, curious to test her reaction to him. Wrapping her arms around his neck, she slid her fingers into his thick, dark hair and drew his face down to hers. He let her take the lead, giving her full control of the kiss. The instant her lips warmed against his, all doubt fled. Maybe she had the same problem he did. She allowed her head to rule her emotions. But there was no containing this. One kiss and she was completely and utterly lost.

"I guess we do have to go through with this," she murmured against his mouth.

"No regrets?"

"Not a one." She opened the door and stepped across the threshold. Glancing over her shoulder, she smiled. "We have all night to get whatever this is between us out of our systems. With any luck at all, by tomorrow we'll be back to normal."

Lucas shook his head. "Somehow that's not my idea of luck."

LUCAS COLLAPSED back against the sheets. "I don't know about you, but this is definitely not out of my system."

Beside him, Kellie fought to catch her breath. "I'm sure we're close. Maybe one more time?"

Lucas choked on a laugh. "I'm not twenty-one anymore. One more time is likely to kill me."

She sat up, drawing her legs toward her chest and resting her chin on her knees. "This isn't working."

"Funny. I'd have said it was working just fine."

A helpless laugh escaped her. "You know what I mean. Now what do we do?"

He rolled onto his side to face her and traced the silken curve of her hip. "I suggest we keep trying to get this out of our systems."

"No matter how long it takes?" she asked drily.

"Something like that."

She escaped the bed, dragging the sheet with her. Winding it around herself, she shoved her hair out of her face and over her shoulder. It spilled down her back in a tangle of bed-rumpled curls. Lucas levered himself onto his elbow and waited while she paced off some of her inner turmoil.

Morning light slipped in through the windows, licking across creamy skin and providing a backwash that turned the sheet nearly transparent. She was so beautiful, slim-hipped, with long slender legs and a softly rounded figure. He wouldn't call her coltish any longer, not the way she'd been at seventeen. What had been a suggestion of curves had ripened with age, making her even more appealing, if such a thing were possible.

She turned to face him, kicking the length of sheet from beneath her feet. "So, how are we going to handle this, Lucas? I hoped…"

"We both did and it didn't work. Foolish of us to think it would." He kept his gaze trained on her, trying to read her mood. Frustrated. Defensive. Wary. He fought back a smile. And still hungry. "There's no going back to how we were before. You realize that, don't you?"

Her frustration came to the fore, edged with a hint of anger. "Yes, I realize that." She fought with the sheet some more, before knotting it in front of her. "I realize something else, as well. I can't have a public affair with you."

"I agree."

A hint of vulnerability darkened her eyes. "Does that mean we don't—"

"Hell, no. We do. And as often as possible. We're just discreet about it. Eventually whatever this is between us will fade."

Her gaze clung to his. "Are you sure?" she whispered.

It was as though time had reversed and he was seeing a seventeen-year-old schoolgirl standing before him, her eyes filled with impossible dreams. He could see the need in her, the hope, and knew hers were needs and hopes he couldn't possibly fulfill. He didn't have it in him. He never had.

"Don't." He uttered just that one word, but he knew it might as well have been a slap. He came off the bed with a smothered curse and wrapped his arms around her. "How is it possible that so many years can go by, and yet neither of us has changed? You still want what I can't give. And I still want what I shouldn't have."

He could hear the tears buried in her trembling

laugh. "You'd think we'd have outgrown such foolishness," she said.

"Apparently not." He cupped her face and lifted it to his. The tears he'd heard in her voice glistened on the tips of her lashes and he brushed them away with his thumbs. "Truth time, sweetheart. Let's decide right here and now what we want out of this affair."

"You and Jinx are the only two men I've ever loved." A hint of color warmed her cheeks. "Or thought I loved."

"You never knew me. Not really. You created a fantasy, nothing more. This—" His hands swept over her, eliciting a helpless shudder. "This is reality. This physical connection we feel is the only thing we have between us."

"I know." Her smile held a bittersweet quality. "On some level, I've always known."

"Can you handle a physical affair?"

She gave him a clear, direct look, one painfully empty of romantic fairy tales and moonlit wishes. "If that's my only choice, I'll take it."

"And when it's run its course?"

"Then I hope we'll be friends and continue to work together."

He accepted her at her word. "Okay. That brings us to the business end of our relationship."

Her eyebrows pulled together. "We have to find a way of keeping the two separate."

"Agreed."

"I suggest when we're in the office, it's strictly

business. No touching. No kissing. No suggestive comments."

"That's going to be tough."

"It's the only way this will work. Outside of the office…" She shrugged, causing the sheet to dip a tantalizing inch.

"We keep doing what we did last night," he suggested. "I'm sure we'll get bored with each other in a decade or two."

She wrinkled her nose at him. "Or…maybe it'll only take one more time."

Sweeping her into his arms, he dumped her onto the bed again. "In that case, let's find out if you're right."

Instead, all he discovered was how very wrong she was.

CHAPTER ELEVEN

"WELL, FANS, *as we work our way through July and August, we're definitely in the dog days of summer. These are the races when the teams who want to make the Chase had better have shaken out all the bugs and be running like well-oiled machines. Any mistakes now can mean the difference between being in the top twelve at the end of the Richmond race, and being eliminated from the bid for NASCAR NEXTEL Cup's Championship hunt.*

"Back in the lead is Hutch Matheson, closely followed by Lucas Boyce. We don't know what's gotten into Bad, but something at HRI has given the seven-time champ a new lease on life. He's racing like there's no tomorrow.

"After an incredible start to the year, Cole Whaling seems to have stalled in his mid-season bid to run with the top pack, bouncing week to week between that all-important twelfth place, and a nail-biting fourteenth.

"As for Jinx Junior, he's moved into an impressive fifteenth place and seems to have overcome the Hammond Curse—at least for the time being. But a return to Bristol is coming up and everyone is waiting

and watching to see if history repeats itself. Will young Hammond put Boyce into the wall? For Bad's championship bid, we certainly hope not! Stay tuned to find out whether Jamie strikes again, or Bad holds the Jinx at bay."

KELLIE PULLED HERSELF onto the large wooden raft anchored several dozen yards off the edge of the lake and flopped onto her back, fighting to catch her breath. Closing her eyes, she allowed the sun to caress her, knowing that she could only afford a brief time beneath its rays before escaping back to shore and the shade she'd find there.

An instant later, the raft dipped as Lucas hauled himself up beside her. "Where'd you learn to swim like that?"

"Didn't realize I was part fish, did you?"

"Hell, no. If I didn't know we were in fresh water, I'd have thought a shark was after you."

She squinted up at him with an impudent grin. "There was."

He bared his teeth. "The better to eat you with, my dear."

"That's a wolf, not a shark. Though given your sponsor, I suppose that's more appropriate."

He rolled on top of her, shading her with his body. "If I weren't concerned about you getting splinters from this raft, I'd give you my best wolf imitation right here and now."

She wrapped her arms around his neck. "Then take me back to shore."

He gazed down at her as he combed his fingers through the tangled strands of her damp hair. There was an odd light in his eyes, a hunger that never failed to catch her by surprise. "It was supposed to have eased off by now. Gotten old."

"But it hasn't."

He shook his head. "If anything…"

Desperation warred with better judgment. "It's gotten worse."

"Not worse. Amazing. Outstanding. Incredible."

She closed her eyes against the desperate ache of it. The past two and a half months had been the most extraordinary of her life. They'd also been the most painful. Except when their schedules prevented it, not a day went by that she didn't end it in Lucas's arms and in his bed. And every time she found herself there, she waited to see if it would be their last night together. If the burning desire would lessen, would slip less readily into her veins, would flame with less brilliance.

But it never did.

If anything, it had grown stronger each time they came together. As often as she tried to reassure herself that what they felt was purely physical, nothing more, she couldn't deny that there had been changes in their relationship, some subtle, some not so subtle.

They'd grown more adept at reading each other's thoughts and emotions. It was a natural outcome of even a physical relationship, she supposed. They were bound to learn to anticipate one another's reactions. But there were connections and layers building between them, ones that wouldn't have grown if theirs was nothing more than a superficial affair.

He knew it, too. She could see the awareness of it when they were together and at their most vulnerable. Those were the most difficult times of all, when the overwhelming need to expose all her secrets would take hold and it was everything she could do to maintain her silence. But she couldn't bring herself to tell him the truth about their son. Not yet.

If she came clean now, so close to the Richmond race, it might throw his focus. Worse, she couldn't inform Lucas without also telling Jamie. And it was even more crucial that her son keep his concentration where it belonged—on the race track. But the real reason, the reason she found most difficult to admit even to herself, was that she knew it would put a permanent end to her affair with Lucas. Because once he found out that she'd lied to him—blindsided him, as he'd referred to it in the past—he'd never forgive or trust her again.

Just a few more weeks. Just a little longer. Was that so wrong?

He rolled onto his side, tucking her close. "What are you thinking about?"

It took her a moment to come up with an answer that wasn't too far from the truth. "In part, I was thinking about our first night together." Because of Jamie, it was never far from her thoughts. "I want you to know how sorry I am for lying to you about my age."

"The morning after was a bit of a shock."

A wistful smile curved her mouth. "In more ways than one."

"Were you really hoping for marriage, like you said? Or was that your way of escaping your feelings for Jinx?"

"I wanted marriage."

His jaw tensed. "Just out of curiosity, did it matter who?"

"It mattered," she admitted. "I really thought I loved you. But, even if our one-night stand had turned into an actual relationship, when you told me about your father I understood why you weren't interested in marriage or white picket fences or children."

"My father made his choice, one he claimed never to regret."

Her brow furrowed. "But he was a race car driver. And when your mother got pregnant with you, he gave it up."

"In those days he couldn't have supported a family on his winnings."

"So he sacrificed who and what he was."

Lucas shrugged. "And lived his dream through me."

She levered herself onto her elbow. "I never would have come between you and your dream. I've been in the business too long, seen how much racing means to men like you to take it away from you." It was as close as she could come to telling him the truth. "I couldn't do that to you. I couldn't live with myself afterward."

A shadow drifted across his expression. "I would have, you know."

She closed her eyes, so he couldn't read her thoughts

as easily as she read his. "Would have what?" she asked, even though she knew.

"If you had become pregnant, I'd have given up racing for the two of you."

"And come to hate us."

"No." His hand skimmed the curve of her cheek, then traced the curve of her bottom lip. "I would have regretted letting go of my dream. But, I wouldn't have hated you, any more than my father hated me and my mother."

"But you wouldn't be where you are today. You wouldn't be breaking every NASCAR record out there."

"No, I wouldn't. I have to admit, if I'd had to give up racing, it would have been—" He shook his head. "Never mind. It doesn't matter, does it?"

"No," she whispered. "It doesn't matter."

He cupped the back of her neck and pulled her down until her mouth brushed his. "Still…I would have had one hell of a son."

And then he kissed her more thoroughly, blotting out regrets, stealing guilt and pain, and replacing it with a desire so intense it seemed to melt bone and muscle, melding her with the man who held her. Even as she gave herself up to the intensity of his embrace, she could feel the clouds of despair building on the horizon. Soon the summer would draw to a close and the rain would arrive.

And with those rains would come truth and heart-break, because the truth was, she loved Lucas. She'd loved him eighteen years ago, just as she'd loved him during those long, sweet years of her marriage to Jinx. Just as she loved him now and would continue to do so for the rest of her days. She clung to him, knowing that when the time came and he ended their affair, heartbreak would follow as surely as the rain followed the burning heat of summer.

THE HARD KNOCK at her office door had her head jerking up. "Come in," she called.

Cole entered, closing the door behind him. "Got a minute?"

She regarded him warily, a little concerned by the hardness in his eyes and the tautness building around his mouth. "Sure. What's up?"

Instead of taking a seat in front of her desk, he wandered the length of the office, pausing by the floor-to-ceiling windows that overlooked the shop. "I tried to get in touch with you yesterday. Nobody seemed to know where you were."

She strove for a casual air. "I took the day off."

"Bad wasn't around, either."

"Lucas's whereabouts aren't my responsibility," she replied with deliberate indifference. "So long as he takes care of his partnership and sponsorship responsibilities, and shows up at the race track when he's supposed to, that's all that matters."

Cole approached her desk, edging a hip on the edge. He still had an odd look in his eyes, the hazel hovering somewhere between gold and brown. "You and I have never followed up on our contract talk."

Uh-oh. "True." She started to reach for the phone. "If you want to continue that discussion, I'll give Lucas a quick call and see if he can join us."

It was the wrong thing to say. Anger flashed across Cole's expression. "This particular discussion is private."

Exhaustion washed over her. "How many times have we been over this? He's my partner. He has a say in all business decisions, more specifically all contractual discussions."

Cole's hands clenched. "I'm not talking about the damn contract and you bloody well know it!"

"Then what…?" Her gaze jerked up to clash with his and her breath escaped in a rush. "You mean us."

"Of course I mean us." He held her in place with a masculine aggression that spoke of thwarted desire. "Unless there's someone else you're interested in? Is there, Kellie?"

"That's none of your business."

"I'm making it my business. I told you what I wanted during our earlier talk. I want you. I want marriage. I want a family. I can give it all to you. Everything Jinx couldn't." His expression hardened. "And everything Boyce wouldn't."

She fought to hide her reaction. "What are you talking about?" she asked through numb lips.

"I'm talking about the reason you married Jinx. I'm talking about Jamie."

She continued to stare at him, refusing to respond to what she hoped was blatant speculation rather than anything with substance.

"He told me, Kellie. Jinx. He got rip-roaring drunk one night and spilled it all. I'm not even sure he remembered the next day."

"You are way out of line here."

He leaned in and lowered his voice. "Hell, honey. You only get penalized for straying outside the lines if somebody catches you. You, of all people, should know that, considering how far out of the lines you strayed."

"That's enough."

"It's not even close to enough." His gaze softened and he reached out to snag a lock of her hair and wrap it around his index finger. "I'm not trying to start trouble. No one has to find out about Jamie and Lucas. You think I don't know the sort of dilemma it could cause with Food Basket? I've seen up close and personal how conservative that Farmer guy is. He actually had the nerve to call me up and ream me a new one after that bit of fun Jamie and I got into after Daytona."

Anger speared through her. "You damaged Jamie's reputation with that 'bit of fun.' It could have damaged Food Basket's reputation, as well, which is why Leo had words with you. We nearly lost them."

Cole tilted his head to one side. "And if they find out Jamie isn't the legitimate son of Jinx Hammond? If they find out the majority owner of HRI screwed around with Bad Boyce and conceived a child out of wedlock, then turned around and pawned the kid off as Jinx's? How do you think they'll handle that news?"

"Not well." Her tone was stiff with anger. "But FYI,

Jamie wasn't pawned off on anyone. Jinx knew from the start and offered to help me out of a tough spot."

"You think that's the way Farmer will see it?" He shrugged. "I doubt it. I suspect my version's the conclusion he'll jump to, especially since Jinx isn't around to back you up. Considering what a stick Farmer is, I'm betting he'll dump Jamie, despite being best friends with Boyce. I wouldn't be surprised if it ended their relationship. No great loss, if you ask me, but Bad seems to like the guy for some reason."

"That's enough, Cole. What do you want?"

"We still haven't resolved our little problem."

"We don't have a little problem. We have a driver attempting to blackmail his owner."

He grimaced. "Blackmail is such an ugly word. I much prefer to call it a negotiation."

She pulled from his grasp. "Last time. What do you want from me?"

"I told you. I want it all."

She thought fast, gauging various angles before deciding on the best of a bad lot. "I need time."

He shook his head, amusement causing his dimples to flash. "Never try and con a con. They'll see through you every time. I've given you months to make up your mind. Now give me your answer so I can decide what my next move should be."

"Why don't we meet again after Richmond. Once the Chase has been determined, I'll give you my answer."

He took several gut-wrenching minutes to consider her request before nodding. "After Richmond," he agreed.

He leaned in and stole a swift kiss, catching her by surprise. She instantly shoved him away, glaring. "Cut it out, Cole."

Instead of reacting with anger he grinned. "Just sealing our agreement. I look forward to sealing our next one, even more. Maybe we can find a more private place for that."

The instant he left, Kellie dropped her face in her hands. The storm clouds she'd seen hovering on the horizon were fast sweeping in and nothing she said or did could stop them. Richmond. That gave her two weeks, one of which was out in California, where her time with Lucas would be severely limited.

Since she couldn't and wouldn't agree to Cole's "negotiation," that left her only one option. She'd need to tell Jamie and Lucas the truth. Tears escaped, despite her best attempts to control them. And when the truth came out, she'd lose the two people she loved most in the world, because she couldn't see them ever forgiving her for the magnitude of her lie.

LUCAS KNOCKED ON Kellie's office door, taking another second to double-check the itinerary he needed to review with her.

She answered his knock with a distracted, "Come on in."

Once closeted inside her office, he took one look at her and fought to regain his self-control. They'd agreed to keep their personal life out of the office, to separate what they did at night with how they interacted during the day. Over the past dozen weeks, he'd managed it, though it had been nearly impossible. Now, his two worlds threatened to collide and he wasn't sure once they did that he'd be able to separate the pieces again.

She sat behind a desk heaped with paperwork, not that she appeared to be working on any of it. One glance warned that something was seriously wrong. As usual Kellie wore her hair up, but at some point, it had come undone, trailing to her shoulders in loose curls. If it had been any other day, he'd have found the disarray endearing. Instead, he could only wonder who, what, and why, because as soon as he found out, he intended to take apart that who, what, or why, personally.

For the first time since they'd started their affair, he broke his word. He went to her. Crouching beside her chair, he gathered her into his arms. This close, she looked even more fragile, her features delicately drawn, a painful vulnerability lurking in the soft blue of her eyes. He felt as though one wrong word, one clumsy comment, and she'd shatter beyond repair.

"What's wrong?" he murmured.

She shook her head in denial. "Nothing. Nothing's wrong."

"Don't even try that. You look like hell."

"Gee, thanks."

"Who did this to you?"

"No one. Nothing." She attempted to pull from his hold, not that he let her get away with it. "It's just work."

Kellie was lying to him, and the knowledge edged his temper into the danger zone. "Is it Cole?" She simply stared at him, not answering, and he knew he'd hit the bull's-eye on his first try. "What did he do?"

"It's not what he did—"

"Then, what did he want?"

"To discuss his contract. I told him we'd deal with it after Richmond."

"Are you sure that's all?" To his concern, tears welled into her eyes. Alarm edged past his anger. "What the hell is going on? Did he hurt you? Touch you?"

She dismissed his questions with a quick shake of her head. "I told you it wasn't that."

"Then what?"

"Please. I don't want to do this now. There's so little time left."

He didn't understand a thing she was saying. "Time for what?"

Her chin quivered ever so slightly. Then she drew in on herself, fighting to regain her self-control. "I think you should know that everything's going to change after Richmond."

His eyes narrowed. "Why?"

"I don't want to go into it now." She moistened her lips. "I promise I'll explain after the Richmond race."

"Why don't you explain now?"

"If I do…" She shook her head with undisguised desperation. "If I tell you, it'll end everything and I'm not ready for that. Not yet."

He turned that one over, drawing the only logical conclusion. *She was going to end their affair.* While he'd been preoccupied with making it into the Chase and hadn't been paying attention, she'd finally gotten him out of her system. How could he have missed something so obvious?

It was no different than the desperate, teenage crush she'd had on him all those years ago. She'd used him then as a substitute for Jinx. This time she'd used him as a way to recover from her husband's death. The irony of it would have had him laughing under other circumstances. Before this, he'd always been the one to insist on keeping things casual. He'd always done everything in his power to avoid any long-term emotional entanglements.

Until Kellie.

He'd been a fool. Avoiding an emotional entanglement with a woman like her was impossible. There were too many fascinating layers to her. Too many appealing aspects to explore. And he wanted to explore each and every last one.

"Are you sure you don't want to tell me now and get it over with?" he asked. "Sometimes it's better than dragging things out."

"Not now," she whispered. "Please not now."

Even knowing he was breaking the rules, he leaned down and stole a kiss. And then another. To his surprise, she didn't protest. And instead of responding like a woman on the verge of ending an affair, she clung to him, returning the embrace with a desperation that had all his internal alarms going off.

"Kellie—"

She shook her head. "Richmond. After Richmond, I promise."

He wanted to argue, to force the truth from her. Instead, he decided to wait. Wait until he had the time and privacy to get to the bottom of it, before going off half-cocked. Later, when he next held her in his arms, he'd see if he couldn't coax the rest out of her. And then he'd try and find a way to stop her from ending the affair.

CHAPTER TWELVE

"It's finally here, race fans. One of NASCAR NEXTEL Cup's most exciting races. By the time this is over, we'll know which twelve competitors will be in the Chase for NASCAR's Championship…and which ones will have been eliminated. Eight spots are up for grabs and it's anyone's guess who will get it done.

"Over at HRI, Jinx Junior was eliminated for a shot at the championship after a disappointing run at Fontana. Despite that, he's sitting comfortably in seventeenth place in the points and, based on what he's shown us so far this season, should improve on that before the year ends. Jamie recently told us, 'Richmond is my favorite track. I'm hoping to better my finish from this spring.' Since he finished second, we can assume Hammond will be going all out to win tonight's race!

"Last year's champion, Bad Boyce, also had issues in Fontana, dropping him from second to sixth in the points. Even so, he only needs to cross the checkered line in thirty-fifth or better to clinch his spot in the Chase.

"The news isn't quite so encouraging for the man who finished second in the points last year. Cole Whaling is hanging on to twelfth place by the skin of

his teeth. The smallest mistake could knock him out of contention for the NASCAR Championship. Our pit reporter tried to interview him, but the usually accommodating Whaling has been surprisingly camera shy, suggesting he might be more worried than he's letting on. We'll let you know what he has to say if and when we track down where he's hiding!"

"DAMN REPORTER," Cole muttered as he turned off the television. "Hiding, my ass."

Jamie glanced at Stephanie and they both smothered a smile. "Aw, they're just pushing your buttons so you'll go out and talk to them. They figure if they talk trash, you'll fall for it and give them an interview, if only to prove you're not hiding from them." Jamie deliberately paused a beat, before adding, "Unless you are."

Cole spun around and glared at him. "Is that what you think? When have I ever hidden from the cameras?" He folded his arms across his chest. "Name one single time. Just try."

"I can't think of a one," Jamie claimed in his most innocent voice. "Unless, it's right here and now."

Cutting loose with one of his more colorful expletives, Cole stormed from the hauler. Jamie grabbed the remote and flicked the television back on. Sure enough Cole joined the reporter, dimples flashing and began to jaw on about how confident and relaxed he was. How certain he was that he'd be in the top twelfth by the end of the evening.

"That was really bad of you," Stephanie said, giggling.

Jamie hit the mute button and tugged her close. With Cole gone, they tumbled together onto the couch, wrapped up in a tangle of arms and legs. "I can't tell you how guilty I feel."

"Try."

He pinched two fingers together. "This much."

"I thought you two were getting along better."

"We're getting on great. If we weren't, I wouldn't have done that." He flicked her nose with the tip of his index finger. "It's just one of those jokes teammates play on each other. A pie in the face on camera. A water balloon to the head. A food fight in the garage."

She lifted an eyebrow. "Sounds like that reporter isn't the only one who knows how to talk trash in order to get Cole to react."

Jamie slanted a quick glance toward the television and grinned. "I guess he's not."

"I've been meaning to tell you... I'm sorry I couldn't be in Fontana for you."

The change in subject caught him by surprise. "It's okay," he reassured. "I didn't expect you to fly all the way out to California."

"I feel like it's my fault that you did badly," she confessed in a rush.

Concern swept through him. "Hey, that wasn't you. You can't take something like that on your shoulders. It was just—" He broke off, then finished awkwardly, "It was just one of those things."

Her eyebrows pulled together. "You can't still think it's the Hammond Jinx? I thought you were over that."

"I am." He shrugged, not quite meeting her eyes. "For the most part."

"Oh, Jamie."

He tried to sidetrack her with a kiss. It worked for a brief time, distracting them both as they curled deeper into the couch. But when he flopped onto his back, rolling her on top of him, she returned to the subject with dogged determination.

"How can I convince you that you're not a jinx?"

He decided to be honest. Of course, with Stephanie anything less was an impossibility. "Everyone says I've inherited my dad's skill behind the wheel. No matter how often I try and convince myself that you can't inherit a jinx the way you can good reflexes or mechanical ability, I can't help but wonder. Every time I think I've overcome it, something else happens and it starts all over again."

"That's the media talking."

"Maybe because it's true."

She cupped his face and stared at him with fierce dark eyes that were at distinct odds with the softness of her touch. "Now, you listen to me, Jamie Hammond. The media goes on and on about that ridiculous jinx because it's sensationalistic and attracts viewers. It's a…a hook, just like calling every little thing Lucas does 'bad.' They're pushing your buttons on this issue, just like they were pushing Cole's earlier. And it's working because you're letting it."

He nodded, conceding the point. "Even so—"

"Even so, nothing. Both your mother and Lucas have

told you that it's easier to blame everything on a stupid jinx than it is for you and the people on your team to take responsibility for your errors." She thumped his chest with her index finger. "Look at Lucky. He was using the jinx to hide a drinking problem."

"But… Dad believed in the jinx. Heck, he lived it."

"Granted, he had more strife than the average person. But he also had more successes. That's life. It might not be fair, but we each have to deal with the cards we're dealt." She kissed him, a fall of midnight hair sweeping forward to enclose them in their own private world. "I happen to think the cards we've been dealt are pretty special. And I won't have you denying us the chance to learn and grow by blaming all our adversities on a jinx. If it's all a jinx, all up to fate and not up to driver skill, then why bother taking the track? Now, stop being ridiculous and choose how you live your life. You got me, Mr. Hammond?"

He tightened his arms around her. "Oh, I've got you, and I choose you. And now that I have, I'm never letting you go."

"That's good to know, because I'm not letting go, either." Her expression softened. "Drive safely tonight, okay?"

"Even better, tonight I'm going to bring home a win."

"I don't care, so long as at the end of tonight we're together again."

It gave him such a high, having Stephanie in his life, knowing that she didn't care about all the trappings. She only cared about him. He'd been lucky to find her, to have her in his life. And if luck were the reverse side of the "jinx" coin, he'd take it. She was right, of course. He shouldn't believe in the jinx. But how could he not when it had been part of his life—part of him—since the moment of his birth?

Still… If it made Stephanie feel better for him to deny the jinx, he would. He fell into her kiss. And as he did so, his final coherent thought was that he hoped luck would continue to favor him, because there was nothing that tasted better than having good fortune on his side.

"YOU DON'T WANT to go in there," Lucas warned.

Kellie paused, her hand hovering above the knob to the hauler, and glanced over her shoulder at him. "Why? What's wrong?"

"Nothing's wrong. You'll just embarrass the hell out of your son and his girlfriend."

Her eyes widened. "Oh, dear. I was going to wish him luck before the race."

Lucas grinned. "I believe Stephanie's doing that right now." He jerked his head in the direction of his own hauler. "Why don't we go in there and you can wish me luck, instead?"

The suggestion proved too tempting to resist, especially considering it might be the last opportunity she'd ever have. "Please," she said. "I'd really like that."

She didn't care who was watching, and apparently neither did Lucas. He propelled her toward his hauler and inside with impressive speed. "Out," he ordered the team members and staff lounging inside.

They took one look and, to Kellie's amusement, assumed an argument was brewing and about to explode. Instead a very different emotion was on the verge of erupting. The instant the door closed behind the final departing employee, Lucas tipped her into his arms and covered her mouth with his. Heat flashed through her, hot and heavy and thick, followed by a burning need that made her wish for one more night with him before she told him the truth about Jamie. Just one.

The awareness that this might be the last time he'd ever take her into his arms, had her returning his kiss with painful desperation. "More." Her hands swept over his uniform, searching for the fastenings that held it closed. "I want more."

"Easy, sweetheart." He caught her hands in his, lifting them to his mouth for a series of swift, teasing kisses. "We'll have plenty of time for more after the race."

Maybe they would. Surely Cole wouldn't insist on an answer the moment the race ended. She could have one more heavenly night in Lucas's bed before having to tell him the truth. "Tonight. All night."

"Good Lord, woman. You're going to be the death of me." Lucas nuzzled her neck. "But I have to tell you, as far as lucky kisses go, this has to be the best I've ever had."

She groaned, forcing herself to gather sufficient brain cells to respond. "Ever?" She considered the possibility. "You've been in the business a long time. That's got to be a lot of kisses."

"It is," he confirmed. "And my claim still stands."

"Then let me give you one more, just to make sure there's no doubt about it."

They didn't have much longer, and Kellie treasured those few stolen moments, hugging his comments to her like bright, shiny gifts. Even afterward, when she took her usual place on top of Jamie's war wagon, she carried them with her, knowing they'd help her get through the painful time ahead.

She'd thought long and hard about joining Dipstick on top of Lucas's war wagon, but worried about the fallout when Cole found out. Keeping to her usual choice seemed the most diplomatic option. Tonight was a special evening, one she had high hopes for. At least, they were high when she didn't take Cole's ultimatum into consideration. If everything went well, she'd have two drivers in the championship race, and her son with his first NASCAR NEXTEL Cup win. Of course, years in the business had taught her to never expect the best. But she could still hope.

She'd always been fond of Richmond. Jinx had gotten his first win here, as had a number of drivers. She could only hope that Jamie would, as well. The race started well. Jamie was near the front, with Cole not far behind. Lucas had qualified toward the middle and would have his work cut out for him picking his way through the field. Because it was only a three-quarter mile track, he risked getting lapped early if he wasn't careful.

Kellie found her binoculars trained on Lucas even

more often than her son. She only dropped in on Cole every few laps. To her relief, Lucas got up on the wheel right from the start, using the multi-groove passing in Turns Three and Four to pick up spots. But even as she watched, an undeniable foreboding filled her.

Like Bristol, the noise level was incredible, the roar of the crowd and the engines nearly deafening. She'd become attuned to the energy level, both on the track and off, cranked to the max, the power of it rumbling just beneath the surface, desperate for release.

It was as though the track magnified all her inner turmoil and reflected it back at her, and she couldn't help but sense that she teetered on the very edge of control. That it would only take one false move and she'd slam into the wall.

The wreck was coming. She could feel it. And she knew…this was one disaster she didn't have a hope of surviving.

ADRENALINE SHOT through Jamie as he missed the wreck in front of him with only inches to spare.

"Did you see that?" he shouted into his microphone. "Could it have been any closer?"

"Easy, son," came Paps's soothing voice. "Fall in line and stay clear of the debris."

"How's the car handling?" Jamie's new crew chief cut in.

Sandy was more easygoing than Lucky had been, and within just a few races, Jamie had developed an excellent rapport with the older man. He seemed to have a knack for understanding "shading." Instead of getting impatient when Jamie would describe the car as a bit loose, way loose, or loose as a goose, he seemed to instantly grasp the finer subtleties. Even better, he had the ability to take Jamie's analysis and fit improvement to generalization in order to produce a top-notch race car.

"We're soft up front where it counts," Jamie reported in. "Grip into the corners is outstanding."

"Then let's throw four on you and get you back out there," Sandy responded. "Go easy on those brakes. Paps tells me they're already glowing."

"You got it."

The second quarter of the four-hundred-lap race saw an unusual number of wrecks, the worst coming when Davy Ellis tagged the outside wall coming out of Turn Four. Overcompensating in an attempt to correct for the hit, he slid his car across the track into oncoming traffic and took out a half dozen of his fellow competitors. It was another one Jamie narrowly missed and it took a few minutes before he could catch his breath sufficiently to report in.

"Focus, Jamie," Paps ordered briskly. "You have to keep your emotions in check if you want to survive Richmond."

"I know. I know." But the comment stirred a flicker of annoyance. Hadn't he come in second in the spring? He understood the track without being instructed like a total newbie.

"And watch yourself coming out of Turn Two. There's only one hole and there were three of you trying to fill it a few laps back. Better to back off until you hit the straightaway. You're beating them into the corners, so if you can get your nose under them, you should be able to pass without too much trouble."

"I can get back onto the throttle faster, too." Which pleased him no end.

"Then use your advantages, son, and stop screwing around in Two."

"Will do."

"You still have half the race to go. You can do it."

Determination filled Jamie. "I will."

Lap by lap ticked by and he hovered in the top five right up until a bad pit stop dropped him to fifteenth behind both Cole and Lucas. "What the hell happened?" Jamie demanded.

"Catch can got caught," Sandy responded. "I couldn't let you leave the pits until we'd freed it. Better we lose a few spots than you get sent to the end of the lead lap."

"How many laps do we have left?" Jamie asked tightly.

"Enough. Just hold on to your temper and work one car at a time," Paps said.

"That's a little tough with so many lap cars between me and the front." He took his frustration out on the wheel, whipping it back and forth to put heat in his tires. "I'll be lucky if I don't go down a lap, too."

"Everybody take a breath." His crew chief's voice came through his headset as cool and calm as spring water. "This sort of mistake happens more often than any of us like. The important thing is how we react to it. Jamie, you need to do exactly what I say. Take it one car at a time. You lose your temper now, you're going to end up hooked to the end of a wrecker. Got it?"

"I'll do my best."

But frustration ate at him, making him rash in his eagerness to drive to the front. More than once he used his bumper to move someone out of his way. He knew he needed to calm down, but the possibility of his first win dangled in front of him just out of reach, taunting him, and it filled him with reckless abandonment. He didn't care what it took, or how hard he had to drive, he wanted that win. He *had* to have it. More, he intended to get it, no matter who he had to move aside to get there.

"NASCAR's issued us a warning," came Sandy's voice, the tone deliberately detached. "Next time you bang bumpers, they're going to park you for rough driving."

"Got it."

He backed off after that, forcing himself to be patient as he worked his way back into the top five. As the final laps wound down, he took fourth from Lucas, maneuvering around his teammate with exquisite care. Hutch Matheson gave up third to him without too much of a fight. And then he caught up with Cole, who was in second. Jamie waited until they were heading into Turn Two to dart toward a hole that opened up. To his horror, Cole went for the same spot.

They hit with a jarring thud. There was an earsplitting screech of metal and Jamie had just enough time to brace himself before they slid into a synchronized spin straight into the wall along the backstretch. The force of the hit knocked the wind out of him, and he sat, stunned, for a full thirty seconds, feeling sicker than he could ever remember.

He keyed his mike as the full realization of what he'd done sank in. "I'm sorry! I'm really sorry," he stammered. "Did I... Did I knock Cole out of the championship?"

"Are you injured?" He cringed at the sound of Sandy's crisp response.

"No, no." He watched Cole refire his car and limp toward pit road. His own car had stalled and it took him a half-dozen tries to get it started again. "I'm fine. I'm heading for the garage."

"I'll see you there," was all his crew chief would say.

"Tell me about Cole first." He waited for the line of cars following the pace car to stream by, then pulled low on the track and worked his way around Turn Four to the entrance to pit road and the garages.

"He's out," his grandfather announced. "Of both the race and the championship run. He's gone to the garage."

The next twenty minutes were the worst of Jamie's life. The instant he parked his ride in his garage stall, he wiggled out and went in search of Cole. Pit reporters blocked his path, but he shoved his way through them, without comment. He found Cole coming out of the 199 garage. One look warned he'd have been wise to wait until his teammate had had time to cool down. He vaguely saw his mother pushing through the crowd toward him.

"Cole." He approached the other driver, utterly miserable. "I'm so sorry. I didn't mean to take you out. You gotta know that. I'd have done anything—"

"I don't want to hear any lame excuses," Cole snapped, his temper solidly out of control. He grabbed Jamie by the front of his uniform and gave him a hard shake. "NASCAR warned you, you arrogant fool. But you were so intent on getting your first win, you just didn't give a damn who you hurt or who you knocked out of your way."

"We were both going for the same real estate. It was an accident." The words tumbled out, desperate and apologetic. "It was the Hammond Jinx. There's no other explanation."

Cole snarled in fury. "You idiot. In order for you to inherit the Hammond Jinx, you have to be a Hammond."

Jamie vaguely heard his mother's shout. "Cole, no!"

"What do you mean?" he asked, his temper rising. "What the hell are you talking about? I am a Hammond."

"The hell you are. Hasn't your mother told you the truth, yet? You're not Jinx Junior." Cole's mouth curled in disgust. "You're Boyce's Bastard."

CHAPTER THIRTEEN

"EVEN MORE ELECTRIFYING than who made the Chase for the NASCAR NEXTEL Cup Championship is the latest news coming out of HRI, news that has the racing world reeling. Last night in Richmond, during a live broadcast at NASCAR's definitive race—the race that decided who earned one of the coveted top twelve Championship spots—Cole Whaling shocked fans everywhere with a bizarre allegation.

"After being knocked out of contention for the championship by teammate Jamie Hammond, Whaling claimed NASCAR's youngest driver is actually the son of Lucas 'Bad' Boyce, rather than the late great Jinx Hammond.

"Let me tell you, it was sheer pandemonium down in the garages. Never have I seen anything this unbelievable. Immediately after the wreck that took Cole Whaling out of contention, he and young Jamie had a physical confrontation during which Whaling made his shocking accusation. The minute the race ended, Lucas 'Bad' Boyce joined in the ruckus.

"At some point during the altercation, Kellie Hammond was shoved to the ground, while Boyce and

Whaling nearly came to blows. In fact, they would have if Boyce's quick-thinking team hadn't forcibly removed him from the scene, no doubt saving him a hit in the points that could have knocked him back out of the NASCAR Championship!

"Young Hamm—Boyce... Frankly, folks, I don't know what to call young Jamie, anymore, but one thing's for certain, the boy was shell-shocked by Whaling's allegation. So was his mother, Kellie Hammond, who sustained unspecified injuries as a result of her fall.

"Once again, teammates for all parties came to the rescue, whisking the key players from the scene before we could get any further comment about the truth of Whaling's claim. The media is currently camped outside the Hammond compound awaiting an official statement. As soon as we have more information, you'll have more information. So stay tuned to what was once a stock car event and has now become a demolition derby!"

"IS IT TRUE?"

Kellie flinched. They were the same words her son had uttered right before Lucas had stalked unannounced into her study. There hadn't been time for a conversation with either of them before this. Last night she'd been rushed off to the medical center after her fall, a fall she didn't think either Jamie or Lucas knew about. From what she'd been told, all three teams had then snatched up their respective drivers before matters could turn any more ugly and removed them—willing, or otherwise—from the racetrack.

The only good news resulting from the night's disastrous events was that Lucas had ended the race in second, clinching a third-place berth in his championship bid. The not-so-good news was he'd been ambushed by reporters the instant he'd climbed out of his car, everyone clamoring to know if the bombshell Cole had dropped was true. Was Lucas the biological father of Jamie Hammond?

It had been horrible to watch the interview, repeated over and over on all the sports stations. First there'd been that look of confusion, followed by dawning comprehension. Finally had come the biting anger. Through it all, through all the questions and accusations and insinuations, he'd kept his cool and hadn't said a word. But then, words hadn't been necessary, not when his expression said it all. At that point, he'd hurdled the pit wall and raced toward the garages, and into the middle of the ensuing skirmish with Cole.

"Well? Is it true?" Lucas repeated.

This time she didn't hesitate, but gave it to him straight and unvarnished. "Yes, you're Jamie's father."

"No!" Jamie shouted. "It's a lie. Jinx is my dad."

Tears pressed for release and Kellie forced them back. "Jinx was your dad," she told him as gently as possible. "He'll always be your dad. But Lucas is your biological father."

"Why?" Lucas asked. That one acrid word contained all the anger and disillusionment and betrayal he felt.

Jamie turned on him. "Maybe I should be asking you

that question. Why? Why did you desert my mother?" His lip curled. "Oh, let me guess. You didn't have time for a wife and family. You were too busy being The Big Bad."

"Stop it, Jamie." If she could have stood without betraying her injuries, she would have. Instead, she continued to sit, aware that she appeared too casual. Too uncaring. "I never told Lucas I was pregnant."

Lucas trained his gaze on her, his eyes two green pits of fury. "Which brings us back to my last question. Why didn't you come to me when you found out you were pregnant? I asked if it was mine. You denied it."

"Because of what you told me about your father." She turned her attention to Jamie, willing him to understand. "Lucas's father gave up a promising racing career when his mother became pregnant. I couldn't allow history to repeat itself."

"He didn't have to throw us away like so much garbage. He could still have raced," Jamie insisted. "He's good. Hell, he's great. He makes more than enough money to support a wife and baby, if he wanted."

"Not in those days. Not when he was first starting out." She leaned forward. "Honey, I was seventeen. Foolish. And I made a mistake. But one wonderful thing came out of it. You. When Jinx found out I was pregnant, he offered to marry me, to claim you as his own. He loved you, Jamie. He couldn't have loved you more if he'd fathered you himself."

Tears glistened in her son's eyes. "You should have

told me," he whispered brokenly. "You should have told me the truth."

After shooting Lucas a look of intense dislike, he spun around and ran from the room, slamming the door behind him. She couldn't have followed him, even if she'd wanted, not with her ankle the way it was. She glanced in Lucas's direction and flinched at his expression. She'd never seen him so hard or cold.

It was the moment she'd been dreading for months. Even so, she faced it squarely, taking full responsibility for eighteen years' worth of mistakes. "I'm sorry, Lucas. Jinx tried to convince me to tell you when I found out I was pregnant. But I wouldn't hear of it."

"I understand. You wanted revenge because I refused to turn a one-night stand into happily-ever-after."

"That's not true. At least, not the part about my wanting revenge. As for the rest of it…" She shut her eyes for a brief instant. "I'd lost my mother when I was eight. I was raised in the garages by my father. More than anything I wanted the dream—a husband and children and a pretty little house. To be a grown-up woman instead of the team's grease monkey. I didn't realize until the next morning that my dream was your nightmare." She held out her hand in appeal. "Don't you see? I was alone and frightened and not thinking straight."

"You should have told me," he stated implacably.

She tried again, tried to explain the irrational thinking of a teenage girl who'd found herself dealing with adult issues far beyond her emotional ability to handle. "You were good, one of the best drivers I'd ever seen. Because of Paps, I'd been around racing long enough to know just how good. How could I ask you to give that up?"

"By doing just that." A bitter anger ripped through his words. "You could have asked. Given me a choice. Instead, you made the decision for me."

She had to know. "And if I had come to you, what would you have done?"

He didn't hesitate. "The same as my father."

His response didn't surprise her. He'd told her as much that day at the lake. "Exactly. Which is why—"

He cut her off with a swipe of his hand. "It was my decision to make. You took that away from me." His voice turned gritty. "Damn it to hell, Kellie. You took my son from me and allowed another man to raise him. You allowed my son—*mine*—to call another man 'dad.' How could you do that to me?"

He was killing her, inch by inch. And she deserved every cutting word of it. "I thought that if you'd picked me, picked Jamie over racing, you'd have resented us for the rest of your life."

He withdrew, closing down emotionally. One minute his face was alive with pain and the next it became a blank slate. "We're never going to agree on this issue, Kellie."

He was right, so instead she asked the question she'd been dreading. "Where do we go from here?"

"Nowhere."

She'd expected his answer, had known what it would be from the instant she'd realized she'd have to tell him the truth. But that didn't lessen the heartache.

When she remained silent, he said, "At some point we'll discuss how best to handle HRI since we don't have any choice but to deal with each other on a business footing. But from now on, there is no us. Not anymore." He didn't give her time to do more than absorb the blow, before saying, "I do have one question, just out of curiosity."

She fought to respond, to keep things as calm and unemotional as Lucas. "What is it?"

"How did Cole know? Did you tell him?"

She hadn't thought the pain could be any worse, but that single question proved how wrong she'd been. "I didn't even tell my own father." Her voice broke and she clenched her hands as she fought to regain control. "No, I didn't tell Cole. According to him, Jinx got drunk one night and was indiscreet."

"So Jinx told Cole, but you never told anyone, not even your own father." Lucas's eyes narrowed. "You sure he doesn't know? It would explain a lot about his attitude toward me."

"He…he told me recently that he's always known that Jinx wasn't Jamie's father. But I don't think he realized you were the one until you joined HRI." She shifted, biting back a moan when she accidentally jostled her ankle. The rest of her comment escaped in a breathless rush. "When you get past the difference in hair and eye color, you two look quite a bit alike, right down to your mannerisms. Dad saw it straight off."

"You've gone pale. What's wrong?" He crossed to

the couch and crouched down beside her. Gently he probed her ankle, jerking his hand away at her helpless reaction to the pain. "What the hell happened?"

"I fell when that scuffle broke out between the three of you last night."

He swept her hair back from the side of her face, revealing the bruise that ran along her temple. "Fell? Or got hit? Knowing you, I'm guessing you tried to wade in and break things up."

She shuddered beneath his touch, filled with reawakened desire. She fought to hide it from him. Lucas would never forgive her betrayal, he'd made that clear enough. Allowing herself to want so desperately would only prolong the agony of their parting. "Hit. Then fell."

For a brief instant his hand drifted along the curve of her cheek, and the caress, one between lovers, spoke of intimacy and longing and need. And then he pulled back, the heat of his touch replaced by cold rejection.

"We still have ten races to get through," he said.

"What happens then?"

"Either we put our personal issues aside and find a way to remain business partners. Or I collect my marbles and go home."

"Do you really think we can keep our relationship strictly business?"

"I won't have a problem with that." He lifted an eyebrow. "Will you?"

Her answer escaped before she could prevent it. "Yes."

"Then I suggest you find a solution to that problem, because from now on, that's all we are."

The instant he left, she burst into tears. She'd known this day was coming and had dreaded it, had dreaded the moment when the sparks that had ignited between them would be doused before they could fully flame anew. She'd waited too long to tell him the truth. Had waited too long to explain it to her son. And now she'd pay a hard price for what the two men in her life viewed as a betrayal.

A light tap sounded at the door and her housekeeper stepped in. "Excuse me, Kellie, but your lawyer is on the phone."

She swiped at her damp cheeks and struggled to regain her composure. "Could you take a message please?"

"It's the third time Mr. Leroy has called." The housekeeper held out the cordless phone. "He says it's urgent and won't take no for an answer."

Concerned, Kellie took the phone. "Fred? What's the problem?"

"I'm sorry to bother you when you have so much to deal with right now." She gave him full points for his tactful way of referring to the events from the night before. "It's about the contract between Jinx and Mr. Boyce."

She shifted without thinking and fought back a gasp of pain when the movement jarred her ankle. "What about it?"

"After I heard last night's news report, I decided I should pull out the contract and go over it, in case you needed specifics about any of the clauses."

"Delicately put, Fred," she said drily. "I assume you

found something in one of the clauses I should know about?"

"Not exactly. I discovered that Jinx never signed the final version. I think it was during that last episode that put him in the hospital. I don't know how it got overlooked," he fussed. "It's never happened in the thirty years I've been practicing law. But rest assured the person responsible will be dealt with most severely."

"Wait a minute. I don't understand. Are you saying the contract is invalid?" she asked in disbelief.

"That's exactly what I'm saying."

THE NEXT FOUR WEEKS passed with everyone maintaining a wary distance. The teams made a point of avoiding each other, as did the drivers. The fallout from Richmond had seriously affected all their performances. Lucas had dipped to a dismal eighth in the points, and for the first time ever, he struggled with his focus.

He could also tell that Kellie and Jamie hadn't worked through their issues. Of course, four weeks wasn't nearly long enough for something of this magnitude. But it was obvious to even the most casual observer that the teenager was struggling to come to terms with what he'd learned.

Although he didn't attack each race the way he had at Richmond, Jamie picked up a reckless aggressiveness that hadn't been there before, both on and off the track. The only good that came out of the entire situation was that some of the older drivers, who'd accused Jamie of a certain arrogance and disrespect, had changed their tunes, no doubt sympathizing with the emotional upheaval the boy was experiencing.

To Lucas's surprise, Cole chose to approach him at the Charlotte race, in full view of the cameras. Up until then, the two of them had been careful to keep as far away from each other as possible. Over the weeks, their anger had cooled, but Lucas suspected it wouldn't take much to push it into the danger zone again.

"Yeah, yeah. I know," Cole said as he approached. "What the hell am I doing here?"

Lucas folded his arms across his chest. "That would be my first question."

Cole leaned his hip against Lucas's car. "And my answer is, I felt you deserved a warning."

"A warning." Lucas cocked an eyebrow. "What sort of warning?"

"It's about your contract with Jinx."

There was a sly, calculating look in his teammate's gaze, one that made Lucas want to rip the dimples right out of the other man's face. "Last time I checked that was none of your business."

Cole shrugged. "Still isn't. But that won't stop me from telling you that there's a loophole in your contract somewhere that your lawyers apparently overlooked."

How the hell could he know that? "Bull."

"I'm serious, man. According to my sources, Kellie can negate the contract and there's not a damn thing you can do about it."

"And I'm supposed to believe you...why?" He

snapped his fingers. "I know. It's because you're so honorable and trustworthy."

Cole shrugged. "Believe me or not, I don't particularly care. I just felt I should give you the heads-up."

"Out of the goodness of your heart."

"Hell, no. It's a win-win situation for me." Cole ticked off on his fingers. "If Kellie uses the loophole, you're out on your butt, which means I win. And if Kellie doesn't use the loophole, I still win."

Lucas chewed on that one for a moment. "How is that a win for you?"

"It's a win because I get to be the one to tell you that your contract's invalid." Cole grinned. "I gotta say, I'm thoroughly enjoying myself here. And since NASCAR's watching you can't even deck me."

"Watch me."

"Don't forget the NASCAR Championship, bubba. You've already dropped to eighth. You wouldn't want to lose any points, would you? Especially not because of me."

Lucas ground his teeth together. "When this is over—"

"Yeah, yeah. Send me the memo." Cole scratched the side of his nose with his middle finger. "And here's mine right back at you."

Lucas saw red, and it took every ounce of control not to punch the other driver. "One last question."

"Shoot."

"How do you know about the contract? Did Kellie tell you?"

That earned him another dimpled grin. "I guess I could really try and rattle you and claim she did."

Relief shot through Lucas. "But she didn't."

"Nope."

"Then how—"

Cole winked. "I'm no dummy, despite my image. I'm banging fenders with the law firm's legal secretary."

TWILIGHT SETTLED OVER the Hammond compound, bringing with it a fall crispness to the late-October air. They'd just come off Atlanta with a season-defining win that had catapulted Lucas back up into the top five in the championship hunt. After gathering to celebrate and plan their strategy for Texas, his team had all gone home, while Lucas had taken the hour of solitude to clear up a few business matters.

As he headed toward his Jag, a small sound caught his attention and he paused, peering into the dark. "That you, Jamie?"

"Yeah."

Lucas caught the dejected tone of the boy's voice and didn't hesitate. He altered his course and found Jamie sitting on the fence that separated the shops from the Hammond homestead. "I thought I'd find you celebrating after that finish you pulled off in Atlanta. Where does that put you in the points? Thirteenth?"

"Fourteenth. One behind Cole."

"Three races still to go. You can take him."

"I plan to." A hint of anger rippled through Jamie's voice. "I'd stuff it down his sorry throat if I could."

"I'm right there with you." Lucas vaulted onto the fence next to his…son. He was still struggling to get used to their true relationship. "We haven't taken time to talk since Richmond."

"Nothing much to say."

"I'm not sure I agree." He needed to go slow, feel his way carefully. If he screwed this up now, it might be years before he had another chance to bond with his son—if ever. "I wanted to give you some space and let you come to terms with all this before I approached you."

"All this," Jamie repeated. A hint of bitterness underscored his words. "Interesting way of putting it."

"How would you like me to put it?"

Jamie dropped his head. "I'd like it to all go away," he muttered. "I'd like to pretend it never happened."

"But it did. And we're going to have to deal with it."

Jamie turned to look at Lucas. His eyes were hauntingly identical to his mother's, the color the same shade of Texas bluebonnet, with the same burning intensity. "You're not my father," he stated with painful directness.

"I understand you feeling that way. And I'm not trying to replace Jinx. I couldn't." He nearly winced at the sheer misery he read in the teen's face. "That doesn't mean I wouldn't like to have a relationship with you. As adults."

It all hung in the balance for an endless moment, swaying between acceptance and rejection. Until that instant, Lucas didn't realize how desperately he wanted Jamie in his life.

Finally, the boy nodded. "I...I wouldn't mind that." An endearing awkwardness gripped him. "You're not going to expect me to call you 'Dad,' are you? Because that's not happening."

The question stirred a bittersweet longing. He had a son, a son he'd never known. What would it have been like to have been there for his birth? To have watched him grow from toddler to rambunctious schoolboy to a teenager teetering on the brink of adulthood? He'd missed so much, so many years he could never recover.

Lucas took a deep breath. He could resent that loss, and lose still more opportunities. Or he could accept it and move on, build a bridge between them that would stretch into the future. He held out his hand. "Why don't we stick with Lucas?"

Jamie took his hand in a firm shake. "Okay."

They sat silently for a minute. From deep inside the shop a door banged and a minute later Kellie appeared. Oblivious to their presence, she strode across the compound on her way to the main house. Her ankle was almost completely healed, Lucas noted. Barely a limp remained.

The minute she was out of earshot, Jamie asked, "She really didn't tell you about me?"

"No."

"She said that if she had you'd have given up racing for me."

"I would have, yes."

"Oh." Another pause, and then, "Do you suppose

my dad sold you some of HRI so we'd all be together? Do you think he hoped we'd find out the truth?"

Lucas had spent many an hour thinking long and hard on that very question. Each time he'd come to the same conclusion. "I think that's exactly what he was trying to do."

"She never would have told, would she?" A hint of bitterness crept back into Jamie's voice. "If Cole hadn't spilled it, she'd have kept the truth from us."

Lucas shook his head. "You're wrong, Jamie. She would have come clean. I knew there was something eating at her, but she wouldn't tell me what it was. If I were a betting man, I'd say she decided to wait until the end of the season so it wouldn't distract us from our racing. But then Cole moved up the deadline."

"Are you still mad at her?"

"Yeah."

"Me, too."

Lucas smiled. "I was madder four weeks ago. But now…not so much."

"Me, too. I guess it's because I'm getting used to it." Jamie peered at him through the darkness. "Why aren't you still mad?"

"Because before I didn't have a son," he said simply. "And now I do."

"Weird, huh?"

"Very."

CHAPTER FOURTEEN

"WELL, NASCAR FANS, it's the final race of the season! When we leave Homestead, we'll have crowned a new champion. Will the current points leader, Hutch Matheson, be the one? Or will Lucas 'Bad' Boyce pull off a record-breaking eighth NASCAR NEXTEL Cup Championship?

"Mathematically, we're down to those two still eligible to take that top spot. But in order to pull off the next-to-impossible, Bad will have to win the race, and Hutch will need to have some incredibly 'bad' luck. Anything less and Hutch rides home with the biggest win in motor sports. Stay tuned, race fans! We have a feeling it's going to be a bumpy ride."

KELLIE SWITCHED OFF the television with a grimace. "Lucas only has to win if Hutch finishes in the top ten. Can't they get anything right?"

Jamie leaned back against the couch cushions, cradling a cup of coffee. "Relax, Mom. Dip has it figured out. He'll keep Lucas updated." He took a quick gulp of coffee, eyeing her through the rising steam. "Are you going to mind?"

It took her a minute to switch gears and grasp his

reference. "You mean, will I mind if Lucas wins the championship?"

"Yeah."

"It'll be a tough transition." More for her than anyone else, especially since it meant keeping their relationship strictly business, when she wanted so much more. "But no, I won't mind."

Jamie stood, took a final swallow of coffee, and set his emptied mug in the sink and splashed water into it. Bracing his hip against the counter, he faced her. The stance reminded her so much of Lucas it stole her breath and intensified that ever-present ache. "I need to ask you something."

"About your father?"

He nodded. "I need to know why you never told me the truth. I can understand why you didn't tell Lucas." He still couldn't bring himself to refer to Lucas as his father, she noted. "But why did you let me think Jinx was my dad for all those years?"

"Because he was," she said simply. "In every way except by blood."

Jamie gave her a thoughtful look. "Dad sold HRI to Lucas so you'd be forced to tell both of us the truth, didn't he?"

"Yes." She released her breath in a sigh, over-whelmed by regret. "I'm sorry, Jamie. I should have told you. I kept putting it off because the timing never seemed right." She shook her head. "I don't know. Should I have done it right after we'd buried Jinx? It would have been cruel."

To her surprise he didn't react with the pain and anguish he had every other time she'd attempted to broach this subject. For the first time it gave her hope. "Why not tell me once the season started?" he asked.

She shrugged. "I think you can guess. I felt it would have distracted you and you were dealing with enough distractions."

He nodded. "That's what Lucas said."

She took a deep breath and admitted, "To be honest, Jamie, I didn't want to tell you. I was afraid."

"Afraid?" He gave a little laugh. "Of what?"

She closed her eyes for a brief instant before fixing him with a direct look. It was time to open her heart to him, to treat him like the man he'd become, instead of the boy she'd cherished for so many years. "I was afraid you'd hate me."

He stared in dismay. "Hate you?"

"I made a mistake all those years ago. Only it wasn't a mistake because it gave me you." She fought back tears, unwilling to surrender to the blatant weakness of them. Even more, she refused to use them as an emotional weapon against her son. "First I wanted to wait until you were older and mature enough to handle the information. And then I told myself I needed to find the perfect moment to tell you, when there weren't any distractions or crises or…I don't know…work problems. Before I could, Jinx got sick and… I'm making excuses, I know, but it's haunted me all these years. I knew you would be angry and hurt or maybe even—" Her voice wobbled precariously. "Maybe even disgusted with me. So I hid it from you."

"Mom, I could never be disgusted with you." He said it with heartbreaking gentleness. "I was angry and hurt because I found out in such a public way, because you didn't tell me privately."

"And if I had?" She twisted her hands together. "What then?"

He took a minute to think it through. "I'd have still been hurt, mainly because I'd have felt you and Dad should have told me the truth from an early age. But I wouldn't have been angry. At least, not at you. I'd have been mad at Lucas for deserting you. Us." He struggled for the right words. "And I'd have been thrown because I'd have lost myself for a time."

She frowned in confusion. "I don't understand."

"I've always been Jinx Hammond's son. All of a sudden I'm not anymore." He thumped a fist to his chest. "The assumptions I have about myself, the knowledge of who and what I am, are suddenly blurred. It's like driving into the corner and having the car jump out from under you. One minute you've got control and the next you're in the wall."

Her heart went out to him. "Oh, Jamie. I'm so sorry."

A quick smile broke from him. "One good thing came out of it."

Her own smile quivered in response. "What's that?"

"At least I know that any mistakes are my own fault rather than the result of some stupid jinx."

She blinked in surprise. "And that's a good thing?"

"Heck, yeah!" He stared at her as though she'd lost her mind. "You can fix mistakes. Learn from them. Improve. But you can't outrun a jinx. One's skill or lack of it. The other's just the roll of the dice. I'd rather think my fate's in my own hands, not at the whim of some stupid jinx."

It made perfect sense. "What about being the son of Bad Boyce? Isn't that almost as difficult to deal with as a jinx?"

To her surprise, she realized he'd already thought that one through. He nodded. "It's going to be tough. I have big shoes to fill."

She held up a hand. "Stop right there. The only shoes you have to fill are your own. You may be Lucas's son, but you're your own man with your own unique skills and talents. You can choose to live in your father's shadow. Or you can step out and be your own person."

Jamie nodded. "Lucas told me pretty much the same thing."

"Did he?" Warmth filled her. "You two have worked things out, haven't you?"

"He's okay."

High praise coming from her son. "I'm glad."

He shot her a keen look. "What about you? Have you worked things out with him?"

She managed a reassuring smile. "Not yet."

"But you will, right?"

She hesitated. "You realize that Lucas has the option to terminate his contract with HRI, that he can elect not to continue his partnership. If he wants out, he can get his money back and walk away."

"Is that what you want him to do?"

Kellie shook her head. "I want him to stay."

Jamie grinned. "If he wins the NASCAR Championship, he'll have to stay, won't he? He'll own fifty-one percent. How can he walk away from that?"

"I don't see how he can."

More than anything in the world, she prayed he wouldn't. Because if he stayed, it gave her hope, hope that one day they'd be able to work through their differences. And when he found out about the contract and how she'd handled the loophole? a small voice asked. She didn't have a clue how he'd react to that. Maybe he'd understand. She closed her eyes. Or maybe not.

KELLIE FOUND she couldn't allow Lucas to run the last race of the season without talking to him first. Though they'd engaged in any number of business discussions since that disastrous night in Richmond, not once had they touched on the personal. The one time she'd tried had been met with such a stony silence that she hadn't dared bring it up again.

She found him beside his car, all alone, for a change. "Do you have a minute?" she asked.

"Sure." He lifted an eyebrow. "What's our latest problem?"

"This isn't about business."

"Kellie—"

She wouldn't let him brush her off. Not this time. "This won't take long." She gazed up at him, opening every bit of herself and holding nothing back. "You've accused me of blindsiding you. You've said that you can't trust me. And I understand why you feel that way. I *have* blindsided you. I have betrayed your trust. I've put you in the wall, and I've done it on more than one occasion."

"Including recently."

That stopped her. "Recently?" Her brow furrowed. "You mean since Richmond?"

"Cole told me our contract was invalid. My lawyers confirmed it." He cocked his head to one side. "I assume once this race is run you'll hand me my walking papers."

She could feel the color drain from her face. "I'd never do that. Never," she stressed.

A sardonic smile played at the corners of his mouth. "And I'm...what? Just supposed to trust you?"

"I don't know how to answer that." Hurt and frustration ripped through her voice. "And there's not time to convince you otherwise. There's only time to tell you what I came here to say. And it has nothing to do with our contract or HRI or even Jamie."

"Then get it over with."

She stepped closer and fisted her hands in his uniform, not caring who was watching or how many cameras were focused on them, or what conclusion they might draw from her actions. "I love you, Lucas. I fell in love with you as a reckless seventeen-year-old child. And then I fell in love with you all over again as a thirty-five-year-old widow. I fell in love with you at a time when I thought the possibility for this depth of emotion had passed me by. You don't have to love me back. But I refuse to keep pretending that I don't feel it. I spent more than eighteen years doing that, and I won't let another minute of another day go by without telling you how much I love you."

WITH EVERY WORD the muscles in his jaw and across his shoulders tightened. "How am I supposed to trust you after Jamie?"

"You'll have to figure out the answer to that. Do you love me enough to forgive me, or don't you? It's that simple, Lucas."

"The contract—"

She simply stared at him. And then she turned and walked away.

The instant she did, he knew.

She'd honored the contract. Somehow she'd closed the loophole. He knew it as sure as he knew that as a frightened seventeen-year-old she hadn't told him about her pregnancy because she loved him and thought she was doing the right thing. And that she'd kept that secret because she'd been trying to honor her commitment to Jinx and the family bond they'd created.

And Lucas realized something else. He loved her as much now as he had before he'd found out the truth about Jamie, possibly more. Because not two minutes ago he'd seen the true heart of this woman, a woman he'd wanted for as long as he could remember.

There was only one way he could think of to prove it to her. But in order to do it, he'd have to win the race.

THE HOMESTEAD race got off to a clean start, the progressive banking unlike any other NASCAR NEXTEL Cup racing venue. Kellie had made one last-minute change while the cars took their warm-up laps. Instead of assuming her usual position on top of Jamie's war wagon, she sat next to Dipstick and accepted headphones and a microphone so she could listen and talk to her drivers. She didn't know if anyone told Lucas, but she wanted the rest of the NASCAR community to see and understand that she was throwing her full support behind the man she loved. What Lucas might make of it, she'd no doubt discover after the race.

"Hutch has taken the lead," Dip reported. "That's five bonus points."

Kellie shrugged it off. "I'm not worried. If we're going to take this thing, it'll be with a win."

Dipstick keyed his mike. "Watch Turn Two, Bad. I'm seeing drivers washing up the track right in front of other cars. Ellis almost got put into the wall."

"Yeah, I saw it. Listen, I'm a tad loose. Let's think about an air pressure adjustment when I come in."

"You got it."

Through it all, through lap after lap, Kellie watched and waited, and worried. She didn't want this to be her last race with Lucas, but his reaction when he eventually found out what she'd done regarding the contract filled her with apprehension. Would he ever trust her? Based on her last conversation with him, it seemed doubtful.

And most important of all…would he ever love her?

"BOYCE?"

Lucas grimaced and keyed his radio. "Get the hell off my frequency, Whaling."

"Relax. We're under caution. Just listen to me for a second."

"I said get the hell off my frequency or I'll report you to NASCAR."

"Could you shut up for two seconds? There's something you need to hear. Switch over to Jamie's radio."

Damn it! "What's going on, Whaling?"

The other driver laughed. "I'm being the good guy for a change. People listen in on our radio communication, you know. I tell you to stick your ears on Jamie and it helps you, I come across as Mr. Wonderful. Now haul on over there so people can love me again."

It took every ounce of self-possession to take instructions from Cole. But something about the urgency underscoring his teammate's voice had Lucas switching to Jamie's frequency.

His son's voice crackled through his headphones. "No way. I don't care what it costs me. It'll cost Lucas more. He'll lose the championship if I win."

"Listen to me," Kellie's voice cut in. "You have a serious shot at winning this race. You can't worry about Lucas."

"You heard me," came Jamie's stubborn reply. "My mind's made up. I'm not going to change it no matter what you say."

"Do you think that's how Lucas wants to win his eighth NASCAR Championship?" Impatience edged the question. "By default? If that's what you believe you don't know your father very well."

"And you do?"

Lucas winced. Ouch.

"Yes, I do," came her calm retort. "I've loved that man more years than you've been around. And I can tell you with absolute certainty that the only way Lucas wants to win that championship is through his own skill and talent. Isn't that how you'd want the win?"

There was a prolonged silence, and then, "Yes, but he'll also lose controlling interest in HRI."

"Is *that* why you're doing this? So he'll stay at HRI?" she asked in disbelief. "Listen to me, Jamie. Lucas won't lose a thing. There was a loophole in that contract Jinx signed with him. It's not valid. At least, it's not unless I choose to enforce it."

"*What?* What are you going to do?" Anxiety rippled through the airwaves. "You can't cut him out now."

"I signed off on the entire fifty-one percent. It's his as of yesterday."

There was a moment of silence, and then, "He owns majority interest in HRI?"

"Yes. Which means he doesn't lose a thing other than the NASCAR Championship if you win this race. Now pay attention. You get up on that wheel and drive the tires off that thing. You understand? If you don't do everything you can to win, I can personally guarantee that the minute Lucas hears about it, he's going to terminate *your* contract. You got that?"

"Yes, ma'am."

"I need to talk to Cole before the restart. You okay now?"

"I'm fine."

The instant Kellie switched off, Lucas spoke up. "She's right, you know. If you think I want the championship because you've thrown the race, you don't know me very well."

"Bad?" Jamie sounded shocked. "You heard?"

"Every word. Now listen up. No son of mine throws a race. You got that, boy?"

"Got it." There was a brief pause, and then, "Sorry, Lucas. Looks like this is one race you're going to lose."

"We'll see," he said gruffly.

There wasn't time for more conversation after that. The flagman gave the signal for one lap to go. The instant they took the flag, Hutch Matheson, the points leader, jumped high and passed three cars, falling into third behind Jamie.

Lucas had never felt so torn. More than anything he wanted that eighth championship, to be the first NASCAR driver to ever achieve such a feat. But he discovered he wanted something else just as much. He wanted to see his son win his first race.

His jaw tightened. He'd just finished telling Jamie he wouldn't want to win because another driver had thrown the race. That meant he had no choice but to give his son the same respect. It was time to do what Kellie had said. Time to get up on the wheel.

"How many laps?" he asked Dipstick.

"Eleven."

Driving flat out, he pulled up alongside the sixth-place car and passed him as though he were standing still. With ten to go, he grabbed fifth. It took another full lap to catch up with the fourth-place driver. Just ahead, he could see Hutch in third, with Jamie still in second.

If he wanted to get to his son, he'd have to take chances. The cars swept into second and Lucas went three wide. Jumping on the gas coming out of the turn, he darted into third. He could feel the angry push from Hutch right behind him, feel the other driver's frustration. He didn't look back.

Up ahead, Jamie was running side-by-side for first. It slowed him just enough for Lucas to catch up. And when Jamie completed his pass, Lucas followed right behind, taking second.

Static sounded in his ear, and then Dipstick said, "White flag. White flag's in the air."

Lucas motored down beside the Number 56 car and battled his son into the first corner. Jamie washed up ever so slightly, his inexperience showing.

"How far back is Hutch?" he asked Dipstick.

"You have to finish first. You hear me, Bad? Second is no good."

"Got it."

By Turn Two, Jamie had gathered up his car again and charged the corner door-to-door with Lucas. They hit the backstretch with only inches separating the two cars. In Turn Three, Lucas edged ahead by no more than a bumper. But Jamie didn't give up. And this time he didn't lose his focus. Keeping exquisite control of his stock car, he dove into Turn Four and came out in the lead.

Ahead of them, the checkered flag was out and the two cars flashed across the start/finish so close it was impossible to tell who'd won. Lucas could hear shouting in his headphones. And then his spotter clicked on.

"Careful, Bad. They're crashing behind you. Stay high when you come back around."

"Who won?" he demanded.

"Jamie. Jamie took it. Sorry, man."

It was the oddest sensation, feeling the punch of disappointment vying with the thrill of knowing his son had just won his first race. "Got it. Thanks, guys. This has been the most amazing season. I couldn't have asked for any more from any of you. I'll see you on pit road."

He drove up beside the Number 56 car and rubbed his car against Jamie's, scratching a donut in his door in a time-honored way of congratulating the winner. Dropping his window net, he gave his son a thumbs-up before leading the cars that hadn't been caught up in the crash down pit lane. He could see Jamie doing an impressive burn-out in his rearview mirror, the sight filling him with a peculiar sensation—fatherly pride.

Parking his car, Lucas wriggled out of the window. He'd barely gained his feet when he saw Kellie running in his direction. Shoving past the various reporters and cameramen swarming his car, he raced toward her. Reached her. Swept her up in his arms. And then he kissed her, kissed her like there was no past, only a limitless future.

After an endless minute, he pulled back a scant inch. "Let me say this before we get interrupted. I love you, Kellie Hammond."

"I love you, too," she told him between a flurry of kisses.

He caught her precious face between his hands. "Why did you do it? Why did you give me controlling interest when I hadn't earned it?"

"You heard?" Tears flooded her eyes. "You earned it and then some. You earned it by working with me even when I'd betrayed you. And you earned it by trusting me when I didn't give you any reason to."

He shook his head. "Tomorrow we contact the lawyers and we tell them to amend that contract."

Her mouth formed a stubborn line. "I've made up my mind, Lucas. I won't take the fifty-one percent."

"No." He smiled down at her. "But you will take fifty. It's what I was going to do, anyway, if I'd won the Championship."

Her tears overflowed. "Now *that* I may agree to." She looked around in confusion. "We have to get to Victory Lane. Where's Jamie?"

"MOM! LUCAS!" Jamie came flying across pit road, throwing his arms around them. "I did it. I won my first race."

"What are you doing here?" She gave him a fierce hug. "You're supposed to be in Victory Lane."

"Not without you two. I want my family with me." He pulled back, beaming at them. "I won. I really won."

Lucas slung an arm around his neck and knuckled the top of his head. "Congratulations, Jamie. That was one of the best races I've ever been a part of. There's not another driver out there that I'd rather lose to."

With undisguised jubilance the three of them crossed to Victory Lane where a crowd awaited. The instant they appeared, cheers erupted. Someone opened a bottle of champagne, spraying it in great arching loops until they were all drenched.

Jamie held off the reporters and officials and searched the jumble of friends, team and press until he found the one face he'd been looking for. Grabbing hold of Stephanie's hand, he pulled her into the circle of his family. And then he fulfilled the dream of a season.

Sweeping her into his arms, he kissed her, kissing her with all the passion of a man who'd found true love. "I've been planning this for a long time," he told her when they broke apart.

She laughed up at him. "What? Winning your first race?"

He shook his head. "Kissing you in Victory Lane." Her blush made his heart swell. "I don't think this moment could be more perfect."

A reporter thrust a microphone into his face. "Jamie, how did it feel to beat your father?"

Reluctantly, he put his game face back on. "As Lucas said to me, I can't think of anyone I'd rather race to the checkered flag. I'm just sorry it cost him the NASCAR NEXTEL Cup Championship."

The reporter's eyes widened. "You don't know?" She turned to her colleagues. "He doesn't know!"

"Know what?" Jamie demanded. He grabbed her arm. "Hey, what are you talking about?"

"Boyce won the championship. Hutch crashed on the last lap. Bad won by three points."

He doesn't know, Jamie realized in shock. "Dad!" He pumped the air with his fist as his father looked over at him. "Hutch crashed. You won. You won the NASCAR Championship!"

It took an instant for the information to process. Once it had, Lucas leaned into Kellie, holding her close. "Did you hear him?"

"Yes, yes. Oh, my God, Lucas!" She threw her arms around him. "You won!"

"Not that." He clamped his teeth together. "He called me Dad."

EPILOGUE

"*WELL, FOLKS, it's finally here again. Another NASCAR NEXTEL Cup Race to the Chase has concluded at Richmond and we have our top twelve finalists.*

"*Cole Whaling returned to the Chase this year, and what a change there's been for this current fan favorite, or Mr. Wonderful as he's now known. First, he shocked everyone when he elected to renew his contract with HRI, apparently working out his differences with his fellow teammates and owners. With a new attitude—a new winning attitude—Cole has helped make the trio of HRI teams unbeatable this season.*

"*Last year's champion, Lucas 'Bad' Boyce, is once again leading in the points and working on an astounding ninth NASCAR Championship. He's had quite the year. Not only is he in a neck-to-neck race with his son, Jamie, but he also married longtime love Kellie Hammond shortly after winning this year at Daytona. The Boyces are expecting the latest addition to their family in early December. Cole Whaling let the cat out of the bag by giving us this exclusive.... It's a boy! No doubt Bitty Bad will prove to be as big a*

NASCAR Championship driver as his father and big brother.

"And speaking of Bitty's big brother… Jamie has also had quite the year. After his win last night at Richmond—a win that propelled him into second in the points, and puts all three HRI drivers into the Chase—Jamie proposed to the girl whose lucky locket he wears each week, Stephanie Farmer. Jamie presented her with a stunning emerald, no doubt to match his Food Basket colors.

"We wish everyone at HRI the best of fortune. Not that they need it. It's clear that the jinx has been broken. And we couldn't be happier!"

* * * * *

For more thrill-a-minute romances set against the exciting backdrop of the NASCAR world, don't miss:

OLD FLAME, NEW SPARKS by Day Leclaire
ALMOST FAMOUS by Gina Wilkins
Available in August

THE ROOKIE by Jennifer LaBrecque
LEGENDS AND LIES by Katherine Garbera
Available in September

A CHANCE WORTH TAKING—by Carrie Weaver
TURN TWO—by Nancy Warren
Available in November

And for a sneak preview of TURN TWO, featuring a cameo by real-life NASCAR driver Carl Edwards, just turn the page....

SUNDAY WAS A PERFECT DAY for racing. Sunny but not too hot, the sky so clear and blue there was no danger of rain, and the air shifted with only a slight breeze. Taylor hoped that a perfect day was a good omen for Hank's first NASCAR NEXTEL Cup Series race.

She was so nervous she could barely stand still. She felt as proud of Hank as if he was her brother or son, and so nervous she thought she might throw up.

Her driver was fortunately made of sterner stuff. If he was nervous it didn't show. He stood proudly in his brand-new fire suit with the name of the chain of hardware stores sponsoring him prominently identified.

"How are you feeling?" she asked him.

He grinned at her, and she could see the excitement shining in his eyes. "I feel good," he said. "Real good." He glanced around as though he couldn't believe that he was here. "Today is going to be a great day."

They made their way to the staging area where drivers were milling around, each with his PR manager. Fans watched from the perimeter.

Carl Edwards caught sight of Hank and immediately walked over.

"How you doing?" he asked Hank.

"I'm doing fine. Not too nervous." He stood there for a second and asked, "Do you have any advice for the rookie?"

"Yeah. Drive fast. But not faster than me."

They laughed and even that little release helped dim Taylor's stress level. She took a quick glance around and thought that most of the PR managers looked more tense than their drivers.

"Really, what I would say is just, you know, enjoy the moment. I'm guessing you've dreamed of this day since you were a little kid."

Hank nodded. She could picture him hanging around cars as a little guy, watching races, finally getting a chance to try a cart and falling in love with the sport.

"There's a lot more guys who dream of going out there than will ever get the chance. You have to drive like you mean it. Drive with your heart and your guts and all your dreams right out there. Keep your focus and—" he shrugged, looked up at the sky as though for inspiration "—do what has to be done."

"Okay."

"What we do is amazing, right?" He looked like he'd pumped himself up with his pep talk. "This is so cool."

"It sure is. I've been practicing my backflips, in case I win."

Carl treated him to his toothy grin. "Stick to something you can handle. Like a cartwheel."

The picture of Hank in his blue-and-yellow suit, turning cartwheels was so ridiculous she had to laugh.

He appeared to take the suggestion seriously. "Think that's too flashy? Maybe I should stick to one of them...what do you call them? Somersaults."

Carl gave him a mock punch. "You're going to be okay."

Then the drivers were being introduced. She heard Hank's name called and felt another swell of pride. This was it. While he made his introductory lap, she walked back to the garage.

The air was buzzing with excitement. She took a moment to look up at the stands and enjoy the spectacle of one hundred and sixty-eight thousand or so fans all set for one of racing's premier events. The stands were a sea of color. Fans sported racing gear, most of which was in bold, primary colors. It was a rainbow of caps, jackets, T-shirts, coolers.

Hank arrived, looking pretty colorful himself in his brightly hued fire suit. He stood by his car, chatting with his crew chief. Photographers were everywhere, snapping photos from every conceivable angle. Hank, like most of the drivers, did his best to pretend he didn't notice.

As drivers walked by, they'd give him a good-natured shove or mumble something that she assumed meant good luck in some incomprehensible sports-guy speak.

As he continued talking to his crew chief, Taylor was thrilled to see a broadcaster walk by for a quick interview.

"How do you think you're going to do out there today?" Hank was asked. A no-brainer question and one she'd prepared him for.

"I'm going to do my best. I've got a great team behind me, a company I'm proud to race for and sponsors and fans who believe in me." He broke into his infectious grin. "I have to tell you and everybody out there who's rooting for me today that I feel ready for this."

Taylor stood by while he climbed into his car, put in earplugs, pulled on his helmet and plugged it in. She watched him strapping in, putting the steering wheel on—getting ready to go.

When she heard the words *Gentlemen, start your engines,* she thought she might hyperventilate. This was it. Not only Hank's rookie race, but hers, too.

* * * * *

*Available November 2007,
wherever books are sold.*

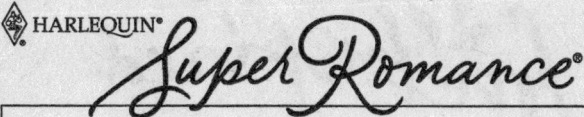

Welcome to Cowboy Country...

TEXAS BABY

by *Kathleen O'Brien*

#1441

Chase Clayton doesn't know what to think. A beautiful stranger has just crashed his engagement party, demanding that he not marry because she's pregnant with his baby. But the kicker is—he's never seen her before.

Look for TEXAS BABY and other fantastic Superromance titles on sale September 2007.

Available wherever books are sold.

HARLEQUIN
Super Romance

Where life and love weave together in emotional and unforgettable ways.

REQUEST YOUR FREE BOOKS!
2 FREE NOVELS PLUS 2 FREE GIFTS!

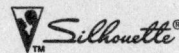

SPECIAL EDITION®
Life, Love and Family!

YES! Please send me 2 FREE Silhouette Special Edition® novels and my 2 FREE gifts. After receiving them, if I don't wish to receive any more books, I can return the shipping statement marked "cancel." If I don't cancel, I will receive 6 brand-new novels every month and be billed just $4.24 per book in the U.S., or $4.99 per book in Canada, plus 25¢ shipping and handling per book and applicable taxes, if any*. That's a savings of at least 15% off the cover price! I understand that accepting the 2 free books and gifts places me under no obligation to buy anything. I can always return a shipment and cancel at any time. Even if I never buy another book from Silhouette, the two free books and gifts are mine to keep forever.

235 SDN EEYU   335 SDN EEY6

Name	(PLEASE PRINT)
Address	Apt.
City	State/Prov.	Zip/Postal Code

Signature (if under 18, a parent or guardian must sign)

Mail to the Silhouette Reader Service™:
IN U.S.A.: P.O. Box 1867, Buffalo, NY 14240-1867
IN CANADA: P.O. Box 609, Fort Erie, Ontario L2A 5X3

Not valid to current Silhouette Special Edition subscribers.

Want to try two free books from another line?
Call 1-800-873-8635 or visit www.morefreebooks.com.

* Terms and prices subject to change without notice. NY residents add applicable sales tax. Canadian residents will be charged applicable provincial taxes and GST. This offer is limited to one order per household. All orders subject to approval. Credit or debit balances in a customer's account(s) may be offset by any other outstanding balance owed by or to the customer. Please allow 4 to 6 weeks for delivery.

Your Privacy: Silhouette is committed to protecting your privacy. Our Privacy Policy is available online at www.eHarlequin.com or upon request from the Reader Service. From time to time we make our lists of customers available to reputable firms who may have a product or service of interest to you. If you would prefer we not share your name and address, please check here. ☐

SSE07

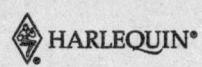